THE BAND
NEVER DANCES

THE BAND NEVER DANCES

J. D. LANDIS

1817

HARPER & ROW, PUBLISHERS

Grand Rapids, Philadelphia, St. Louis, San Francisco, London,
Singapore, Sydney, Tokyo

NEW YORK

Typography by Joyce Hopkins
1   2   3   4   5   6   7   8   9   10
First Edition

Library of Congress Cataloging-in-Publication Data
Landis, James David
   The band never dances.

   Summary: Working through the anguish of her
beloved brother's suicide and trying to forge an
identity of her own, sixteen-year-old Judy goes on tour
as drummer for the hot new rock band Wedding Night
and forms love-hate relationships with two handsome
musicians.
   [1. Rock music—Fiction. 2. Musicians—Fiction.
3. Brothers and sisters—Fiction] I. Title.
PZ7.L23173Ban 1989   [Fic]   88-28401
ISBN 0-06-023721-X
ISBN 0-06-023722-8 (lib. bdg.)

For
Edward B. Landis
Father and Musician Extraordinaire

THE BAND
NEVER DANCES

1

I can remember what it was like before I was born. That sounds impossible, but I can. I do.

I was floating in an endless world. It was dark. It was warm. I couldn't see a thing, and I couldn't even imagine what I would see if I could. I couldn't feel anything either, except the warmth. There was no taste to the food I ate. My fingers met nothing.

But I could hear. I could hear everything.

I could hear the rush of the streets and the song of the radio and the passing of the wind. I could hear the footsteps of people I would never see and the roar of water into the tub and the applause of slamming doors. I could hear voices, always voices, saying things that I didn't understand but saying them in ways that I did.

I got to know people by their voices. My father. My mother. And someone with a little voice, who put his mouth down right to where I was living and made sounds at me and sang songs to me and laughed so much I felt like laughing myself. Maybe I did.

But most of all, even more than my brother's high and happy voice, I heard the beat of my mother's heart. It went on all the time. Whether I was asleep or awake, there it was, sounding around me and through me and in me. *Boom-BOOM. Boom-BOOM. Boom-BOOM. Boom-BOOM.* It was the sound of life to me. It was the beacon of light in the dark night before my birth. It was the most comforting and the most exciting thing I knew. *Boom-BOOM. Boom-BOOM.*

And then I was born. The world rushed in as I rushed out.

The things I heard then!

The joy.

Ever since then I have been trying to make such joyful noise myself.

My name is Judy Valentine. I'm a musician. I blow drums.

2

When you first learn music, you learn to play by yourself. You learn some instrument. It doesn't matter what it is. But you learn it alone, you and your teacher, if you have one. You learn notes. You learn scales. You learn chords. You learn theory. You learn timings. You learn some tunes. Maybe the only thing you don't learn is rhythm. You can try. But if your heart doesn't beat right through your body and into your hands and feet, then you'll never really know what time it is on the clock that rocks.

You play alone. But almost every instrument is meant to play with other instruments. So you search the rest of your life for people to play with.

I didn't want to play alone. I wanted to be part of a band.

And this is the story of how I found my band.

3

I'm an only child. But I wasn't always an only child.

At the time I was born, I had a three-year-old brother named Jeffrey. But by the time I got to be sixteen, Jeffrey had been dead for three years. He died when I was thirteen. He was sixteen. Like me now.

Jeffrey was the most important person in my life. Not my parents. Not my teachers. But my big brother, Jeffrey Valentine, weirdo, freako, nutso, funso.

Sometimes you just luck out. Like when you have an older brother who is your best friend and never for a moment your enemy. Who knows everything and teaches you what he knows, particularly from his mistakes. Who tells you he expects you to be greater than he is and then does everything he can to make you so. Who shows you one way to live and is happy when you choose not to live that way yourself. Who is never satisfied with what he is himself but who tells you that you are wonderful and must be satisfied with who you are. Who is your only real friend in a world where you feel a friend is someone who understands you completely and nobody else comes close to understanding you completely, not your parents, not your teachers, not even yourself.

And sometimes your luck just runs out. When your best friend in the world checks out of the Motel and doesn't even bother to hang a Disturb sign on the door.

Jeffrey's the one who gave me my first drum. You know all those stories. About who gave Miles Davis his first trumpet and who gave Eric Clapton his first guitar and who gave some black dude named Hines his first pair of tap shoes. But a drum! Every kid gets a drum, except it's usually some kind of Indian tom-

6

tom thing or a pair of bongos that turns your palms red and makes you have fantasies about touring with Tito Puente.

But Jeffrey gave me a DRUM. I mean it was a bass drum with a pedal, and it *BOOM BOOM BOOM*ed like some giant human heart trapped in the middle of the earth.

5

Jeffrey was one of those people who never seemed to have to learn anything. I don't mean the petty facts of history or the unbreakable laws of mechanics or even the structure of a flatted-fifth chord. Living. He knew how to live. He was the guy at the House of Life, standing at the front door and inviting everyone in. Everyone except himself, that is.

He looked kind of funny, it's true, but I knew that only because people tended to laugh when they first saw him or to turn away or to ask him what planet he was from. To me he was always the same, no matter how outrageously he dressed or dyed printed messages in his hair or colored his skin so that he would look like no other human being who had ever set foot on earth.

That was during his punk monk phase anyway, pre-punk as far as the world was concerned. As soon as all the kids in London and New York started to imi-

7

tate him, Jeffrey became something else. Jeffrey became ordinary.

"I want to look like everyone else," he told me.

So he wore chinos and plaid button-down shirts and RocSports and argyle socks and a Yankees cap.

"But no one looks like that anymore," I said. "Now you stick out even more than you did before."

"Sticking out is what it's all about," he replied.

"Not for me. I never want to stick out." The total truth. I wanted to know. I wanted to know everything. But I never wanted to be known. I'd been born out of the dark. I'd spent the first nine months of my existence in hiding. It was the natural place for me. Besides, when you had a brother as wild and ostentatious as mine, you were perfectly content to let him front the world.

And Jeffrey didn't insist I be like him anyway. "You don't have to stick out, Judy. I do. But you don't. You're a musician. And the band never dances. Remember that. The band may be right up front onstage, and it may look like all of life is lived within its glow. But the band only plays. It never dances."

I didn't care about all that. All I cared about was finding the band. So I said, "What band, Jeffrey, what band?"

"All in good time, little sister. All in good time."

But by the time that good time came, Jeffrey was something else again, and somewhere else.

Jeffrey was dead.

8

6

The day Jeffrey died I was practicing my drums. We were alone in the apartment. By that time I had a full set of skins, and I practiced them every chance I got.

People think that you have to play loud to practice the drums. You don't. You can play them the way a karate master fights, never landing a blow, or touching his opponent only very lightly, when the fact is the karate master can kill with those very same blows.

Jeffrey loved to hear me practice the drums. He also loved to watch me. He coached me in everything. He opened all the doors in my life.

He wasn't a musician himself, though sometimes he sang to me in a ridiculous high voice, making up the lyrics as he went along. I'd play the drums behind him, even if I was laughing hard enough to make me lose the time.

He insisted I make up my own songs too. But I wasn't as good as he was at being silly. So he made me write them out. That's how he got me into song-writing.

On the day he died, he sang this to me, while I played the drums behind his ready falsetto:

My sister's name is Judy,
She plays the drums a lot,
She thinks she's really cool,
But I know she's really hot.

Her brother's name is Jeffrey,
But so far as I can see,
Jeffrey's only claim to fame
Is that Jeffrey is me.

But if I'm really Jeffrey,
Then what's the sense of this,
I think that I'll stop singing now
And give Judy a kiss.

"Soppy," I said.

"Not one of my best." He blew me a kiss from where he was sitting on my bed.

On the day he died he was in what he called his formalite stage. He wore a tuxedo all the time now, and a pleated, starched white shirt, and a scarlet cummerbund with four little black dress buttons in a row across the front, and a skinny black bow tie that he'd learned four different ways to knot, though it always looked the same to me, and patent leather slip-ons with velvet bows, into which he would slip each morning his newly manicured toes and lightly talcumed feet in black silk socks so sheer that the paleness of his ankles glowed through as if beneath all this finery there were really just a phenomenally elegant skeleton, ready to dance till dawn.

I blew him a kiss back and wiped my brow with my sleeve, even though I wasn't warm right then. It was one of those habits. Drummers were like athletes too. Sometimes I'd daydream I'd have arms like Billy Cobham and play my drums wearing cutoff sweatshirts, my muscles snakes in my arms, my veins strings of lights.

Or should I dress like Jeffrey now?

"I like that look," I said. "Do you think it will catch on?"

"Without question."

"The world will go around in tuxedos?"

"I can see it now. This is the ultimate dress. After this there's nowhere to go. A world of tuxedos. Can you imagine how beautiful it will be?"

"Then why are you crying?" I handed him my towel.

"Beauty always makes me cry. You know that." He wiped his tears with my towel. He never minded my sweat or made a joke about it. Mixed with his tears on my towel, it was the water of life. "Besides, as I said, after this there *is* nowhere to go. That's very sad." He smiled as he said it. "I want to be everything. And there's nothing left for me to be. Do you realize that, Judy? *Nada.* This is it. This is the end. I've tried everything. And after I do something, everybody does it and uses it up. So there's nothing left for me. Nothing. This is the end of the road. The exit. I've used up all my props. I've worn every costume, I've lived every life I could imagine, I've felt everything

11

I can feel. And now I don't feel a thing. And you know what? That's a terrible feeling—not feeling a thing." He motioned for me to play the drums. "A dirge, little sister. Play me a dirge. Like the Ode on the Death of Queen Mary. A funeral march. Jeffrey is taking a walk."

I didn't have any tympani, but I was still able to beat out a slow, sad rhythm on my bass drum and then on a snare.

As I did, Jeffrey stood up and with great formality came over and kissed my cheek. "I love you," he said. "Good-bye."

"Where are you going?"

"It's checkout time."

How was I to know what he meant?

7

While Jeffrey spent the rest of the day writing me a suicide note and then killing himself, I went out to buy a copy of *Pipeline*, where musicians advertised for other musicians to play with them. I always looked for someone who was looking for me: not just a drummer but a girl drummer. As usual, there was no one looking for me.

I wasn't into the club scene then the way I got to be later. I was too young for them to be able to deal with me once it got to be two in the morning, and I was always being asked to leave by some friendly bouncer in a Jesus-and-Mary Chain T-shirt and with tattoos of his boyfriends' names bouncing on his biceps. Also, I couldn't stay up that late. Little girls needed their sleep.

But sometimes I would go in the afternoon, when the clubs were closed for business but open for auditions or rehearsals or sound checks. And I'd listen. And watch. And try to learn. Not how to play. But how to be part of a band. How to behave. What was expected of me. When to lead and when to follow. How to place my drums so I'd be the center of everything, the driving force, and at the same time almost invisible, huddled over my cans in the background, escaping the lights except when I'd raise my head enough to make a halo just above my hot black hair, St. Judy the Divine.

This was all a dream. So far I had no band. I'd never been up onstage, in the lights, blasting away from my hidden throne. But that's where I was headed. I knew it the way I knew the backs of my own eyes.

So I'd huddle small and young at the rear of clubs on summer afternoons or after school or during school, and listen to mostly inferior bands playing music better than they were, or superior bands playing inferior music, and I'd wait for my break.

On this, the day of Jeffrey's death, I went to a sleazy little club way downtown where they knew me enough to let me in and poured me a Tab without my having to ask and took my two bucks without giving me any change and said only two words: "The Zits."

My hands went to my face, naturally, and I prepared to retreat in shame—girls will know what horror crept through my limbs—but the guy who said those ugly little words pointed toward the stage, where a terrible band made up of four white guys in black clothes was just wrapping up a song by playing the same chord over and over, louder and louder, with all the musicians, even the drummer, jumping up and down with each repetition of the chord.

"The Zits?" I asked the bartender.

He confirmed.

"The pits," I said.

He held his nose.

I was feeling really lousy when I got home. But when I sat down to practice, I saw on my drums an envelope addressed to me from Jeffrey. And I was happy again.

Had he finally actually written down a song for me?

Or had he researched possible bands in the area for me to play with?

Or was this just an afternoon note to remind me

that he was my brother and would stand by me always?

Dear Judy,
This is the only thing I haven't tried. I wonder how I'll like it. I wonder how it will feel.

I couldn't decide what outfit I wanted to be buried in. What a monumental decision! And to think of having to wear the same thing until your bones dissolve. Not me! Burn me. And give my ashes to my fans.

You know me. Never satisfied. Dreams— what a huck! I keep wanting to be something different from what I am. A star.

You know what? I don't have anything to be a star at.

But everyone wants to be a star, don't they? So I'm just like everyone else, right?

And I tried so hard to be different.

So what's the answer? Is it better to be different from everyone else? Or is it better to be the same?

When you're different, they laugh at you and ask what planet you're from.

When you're the same, they don't even see you.

Why do I feel there's no me inside me?

Why do I think that when I'm done doing what I'm about to do, I won't feel any different than I feel now?

15

I won't even miss myself.

But I'll miss you. You're the only thing I've ever been good at.

Don't change. Just grow.

Remember, the band never dances. Why don't you dance for a while first? Wait until you're my advanced age before you stop. Study hard so you can finish school early. Then find your band. Find your life.

Is this really good-bye? Or just another outfit?

Love,
Jeffrey

P.S. Please give my best to our parents. Without them, I would not have known you. What a catastrophe! Then there would have been nothing.

P.P.S. Now the only thing left of me is you.

I felt all alone when Jeffrey died. I didn't want to share my life with anyone else. So I shut everyone else out.

I was angry.

I tried to be angry with Jeffrey. But my memories of him wouldn't let me be.

I tried to be angry with myself. But it was as if he were still there, telling me how great I was, telling me it wasn't my fault.

It was our parents I couldn't talk to. And they couldn't talk to me. I never even showed them Jeffrey's letter. I never gave them his best.

I think that when they saw me, they thought of him, their other child, and they felt like failures toward both of us.

And I knew that when I saw them, I thought of him, of Jeffrey, and I felt they had failed both of us.

So we grew distant. We lived in the same house but in different worlds.

Maybe they could still hear my drums, but they rarely heard my voice. And if my mother's heart was still beating, I didn't hear it any longer.

But I did hear Jeffrey. He had told me to dance. So for the next three years, I danced.

I also practiced my drums and wrote some songs— most of them about Jeffrey, like "Brother"—and listened to music, all kinds of music, until I felt my whole body was a sponge full of sound and I was waiting for the hand of God to squeeze the music out.

But mostly I danced. I behaved like a normal girl and went to school regularly and studied so hard to catch up to Jeffrey that I skipped a grade. I talked to the girls and talked to the boys and spent the years between thirteen and sixteen trying to laugh so I

17

could drown out the groans of growing and the silence of the house I lived in and the sound of my own voice telling me that I had somehow failed the person closest to me in all the world, the person I was now going to take care of, the way he had taken care of me, for the rest of my life, for the rest of his life in me.

I danced, all right, but all I was really waiting for was when I got to be Jeffrey's age and I'd have his permission from beyond the grave to go find my band.

And then, one day, Jeffrey and I were the same age: sixteen years, nineteen days.

That was his age on the day he died. That was my age on the day I was reborn.

We were truly brother and sister on that day, twins, the very same age, caught at the same moment in time.

He was no longer my older brother. From that day on he would be my younger brother, ever younger as I grew ever older, until I was sure I would think of him someday as little Jeffrey, my kid brother.

Now that I was sixteen and had been freed by Jeffrey to make my way in life and find a band, I did nothing else.

I graduated from school a year early and with really good grades—Jeffrey would have been proud—and never looked back or went back.

I stopped showing up at home some nights or some mornings if I ended up crashing at someone's flat after listening to music at a club or trying to sit in with some band or listening to records at that same flat and falling asleep, music knotting all my dreams, Mick Jagger the Sleep Fairy dancing behind my eyes, or poor, dead Jaco and Chick, or Sting buzzing me, or all the great drummers of all time, from Gene Krupa to Elvin Jones to Tony Williams to Judy Valentine herself, gently playing to the rhythm of my quiet, sleeping heart. Bringing peace.

I stopped shooing guys away. I needed them around. Some of the clubs got rough at one thirty in the morning, or five in the morning, after hours, when it was illegal to be serving drinks and dancing so your clothes would melt. Men wanted to see into my heart by looking through the holes in my body. So I made some buddies and let them escort me through the claws of the night. But I didn't have to pay for their protection. My flesh was my own. And my sleep. Any guy could come on to me, but no guy could climb onto me. I wasn't ready for love.

I stopped playing solo. Even if I kept living that way.

But it was hard to find my band.

I took out my own ad:

Girl drummer seeks band. 555-8987.

19

All kinds of creeps called. I stopped hauling myself around to audition with them when I got tired of beating them off with my sticks.

So I tried something less provocative to the animal population:

Drummer seeks band. 555-8987.

But no one called.

I started to look at ads again:

Drummer needed for lounge act.
Travel free, costume provided.

Come beat our meat. The Butchers are Long Island's bloodiest band. We need someone to strip our skins. Our power is Raw, our loins are Tender. Come meet our beat.

Brushes only. Cocktail pianist needs sensitive drummer to play classics for insensitive clods. No alcoholics. Gay male preferred.

Chick with sticks our pick. Girl drummer needed to add sass and sex to garbage band, The Acnes, four of the ugliest guys in the Metropolitan area (formerly the Zits). Video contract pending. Ditto Clearasil commercial. Beasts need beauty. Call us, cutey.

The Beetles need a drummer. Come shine our Apple. Reunion of the century. Call Paul or George. (John, we love ya. God bless ya.)

Girl band wants girl drummer. Labia is our name, Sensuarock is our game. Into male groupie scene. "We love it 'cause it loves us so." One-night stands our specialty.

Band seeks drummer.

You couldn't tell a thing from the last ad. It was the only one I answered.

"I'm calling about your ad for a drummer."

"What about it?" His voice was strange, soft, like a whisper, secretive. I couldn't tell if he was young like me or old. He sounded very far away.

"I'm a drummer."

"You sound like a girl."

"I am."

"I don't work with girls."

"I don't work with idiots. Good-bye." But I didn't hang up.

"All right. All right. What's your name?"

"Judy Valentine."

"I thought I knew everybody. Who you played with?"

"The Jeffries." I made it up.

21

"Never heard of them."

"Just two of us. Like Steely Dan." I thought that would impress him.

"I don't like things that are like other things."

"Mr. Originality. What's the name of your band?"

"Suddenly you're asking *me* questions?"

"I've probably never heard of you, either. You or your band."

"Probably not."

"That makes us even," I said.

"Nothing makes us even. Not—"

"You don't know how good I am!" I screamed.

His voice was quiet as he went on after my interruption. ". . . not until I hear you play."

I didn't know what to say. Did he mean I was going to have my first audition? Was I about to find my band?

"You still there?"

I gathered myself together. Down to business. "Where and when?"

"Twenty-nine and a half Lispenard. Top floor. Ring the bell that says Strobe. Eleven o'clock."

I panicked. What was Lispenard? Was that in New York City? It didn't sound like any street I'd ever heard of. And what time was it now? Why didn't I have a clock in my room? Why didn't I own a watch? And what was Strobe? A famous studio that, when he mentioned it, I should have said, "Oh, wow, right, Strobe!"?

"I can't make it that fast," I said.

"Are you planning to crawl?"

"But it's almost eleven o'clock now."

"That's eleven o'clock *tonight*. Not this morning. So rest up. If you're any good it'll be a late one. And one more thing."

Here it came. I was prepared for it. Some dirty thing that was going to keep me away and make me hate him. "What?"

"Come alone. I don't need you to come with some claque."

"What's a claque?" It sounded like a drum from Africa. Where was Jeffrey when I needed him?

The man on the phone didn't seem to lose patience with me. "A claque is a group of people who you pay to admire you."

"I'm a musician," I said. "I'm after the other kind of audience. The ones who will pay to hear *me*."

"If you're good enough," he said.

"I'm good enough."

"As I said, we'll find that out when I hear you play."

"That's right, you will," I said cockily. "So what's your name?" I asked. I might as well know. Right then he felt like my only friend in the world.

"Strobe."

"That's your name?"

"For now."

"Strobe as in light?" I asked.

"Or darkness," he answered.

Well, even if he was the Devil, I was ready to play drums in his band.

I was never afraid of the city at night. But if I were going to be scared, I would have been scared walking from the Canal Street subway station to 29½ Lispenard Street, not because the streets were full of threatening people but because they were empty at that hour of the night. It was an area of warehouses, served by trucks during the day and abandoned at night. I was all alone. I had only my drumsticks to break the fingers of darkness.

Twenty-nine and a half Lispenard looked just like every other building on the block. Large industrial doors with small windows with wire in them. Signs on them to tell you this was where you could come for die tools and Perfect Plywood and wholesale linoleum and Lincoln's Cabin Custom Cabinetry and someone, on the top floor, named Strobe.

I rang the bell and without thinking leaned against the doors so that when the buzzer sounded and they unlocked, I could push my way in before they clicked shut again. But no buzzer sounded. So I rang again. And leaned again. And was not let in again.

Was it the wrong night? The wrong hour? The

wrong place? The wrong Strobe? The wrong band? The wrong drummer?

In despair, I went out into the street to look up to see if there were any lights on the top floor. As I did, I could see coming toward me a tiny fish dying in the air. I didn't move. It bounced off my shoulder, stinging me, and fell into my shirt, down cold between my breasts, and stopped at my belt.

I pinched it out from between the buttons of my shirt. It was a key.

I used it to open the door to my new life.

I climbed five enormous flights of old and cracked wooden stairs that were so high my knees came halfway to my chin with each step. I felt like a little child going up to her room.

I couldn't tell how old he was. He had black hair, but right in the front was a streak of white. It wasn't dyed white; I knew it really grew that way. Something old in the middle of all that beauty. Like his sad eyes in that long, pale face. His deep voice coming from that slim rock body. The way he frightened me at the same time he made me feel I might be able to open up to him.

It was a giant loft. It extended from one end of the building to the other, floor through. Along one wall was what looked like a home studio, with a soundboard and reel-to-reel tape machines and tower speakers as tall as Strobe himself. Along the other wall were living quarters, with an Oriental rug and a tiny kitchen and a round bathtub with a circular shower curtain. There were mattresses along the wall. One after the other. Five of them.

"Who are those for?" I tried to picture him married. With kids. All of them lined up sleeping, one after the other.

"Those are for the band." He pointed to each one. "Guitar. Bass. Keyboards. Vocal." He saved the drums for last. But he didn't say it.

"That one's for me," I said. It was perfect. A band. A home.

"We'll see about that," he said. He pointed toward the studio. The drums were all set up. It was a beautiful set of Pearls, with everything I could want and more than I'd ever had: a bass; a six-and-a-half-inch snare; four tom-toms, ranging from what looked like a tiny eight-inch to a sixteen-inch, two on the rack and two on the floor; timbales; a pair of Zildijan high-hats; a crash; a ride; a crash-ride; and a pang. Off to the side, on a table and hanging from a wooden frame, were tambourines, claves, maracas, triangles, cowbells, gogo bells, and a bunch of small drums like tablas, and mridangams, bongos, and a cuica.

I walked back and forth in front of all these instruments. I could hear them in my mind. My body longed for them. I could feel the energy building in my arms and my legs. My hands started to sweat on my sticks. My skin tingled.

He noticed. "Like an addict," he said. "Look at you. You're starting to jump. Go sit down."

I went behind the drums. He walked away from me.
"What kind of band are we?" I cried out.
He didn't tell me a thing.
I started to play.

12

When I was done, he came up to me and said, "Look,
I know it's hard to play solo."
"Was I so bad?"
"What are drums for?"
"Rhythm."
He smiled. He reached behind some equipment and
pulled out a towel, which he threw at me. It said
"Beverly Hills Hotel." I put it around my neck. It
probably felt like this when you were the losing
pitcher: good to have the rough cloth soaking up your
sweat and rotten over your loss.
"The drums are the core of the band," he said. "The
music is the blood and the drums circulate it. No one
dances without you. That's why I'm looking for a
drummer first. The others will fall into place."
"Was I so bad?" I asked again.
"Who are the Jeffries?"
"The band I played with."
"Drums and what?"
"Drums and . . . my brother."
"What does your brother play?"

"The harp."

Strobe laughed. I could see the muscles in his chest open and close like fingers. "The harp!"

"He's dead."

Still laughing, he said, "The heavenly harp."

He saw right through me.

"He's the only one I ever played with," I said.

"It shows."

I got up to leave. I knew he was right. But how did you get to play with people unless you played with people?

"Come back when you've had some experience," he said.

I stopped and turned around. He had been right behind me. I could see his eyes, two colors, like David Bowie's, except one was purple and one was green. "How do you get in a band if you have to be in a band to get in a band?"

"How do you know how to talk to people unless you already know how to talk to people?" he asked. "You talk to them in your mind," he answered.

"Music isn't in your mind," I said.

He put his hand on my arm and pulled me back into the room. "You're right. Here. Sit down. Let me tell you something. What did you say your name is?"

"Judy, Mr. Strobe."

"It isn't *Mr.* Strobe. What is it, 'Mr. Sting'? Just Strobe."

"Strobe. As in darkness."

"You're threatening my pretentiousness."

"Big deal." I don't know why I said that. He made me more myself, not less, even if he did hold my life in his hands.

"I run the band." He was very serious about that.

"I'm sorry."

"A certain amount of pretense is necessary. The public appreciates it. Show business."

"So how do you think of yourself? I mean, what do you call yourself when you call yourself something?"

"Actually," he said, "by one of my other names. I have a lot of names. I've gone by many names. Jeffrey, for example."

Big deal. Synchronicity. The King of Pain. "My brother's name."

"I know." He looked at me closely, but I didn't know what he was looking for. So I had nothing to give him. "Do you want a hit?" he asked.

"Of what?"

"What's your pleasure?"

"To tell you the truth, Mr. Strobe, I'd rather talk about my playing."

"And you think drugs have nothing to do with your playing?"

"Nothing. The only hit I want is a hit song."

"So you don't do drugs?"

Did he? He looked it. The eyes of different colors. The thin body. The shock of white hair. The luminous skin burned smooth by heroin or spotlights. And there I was, so straight. Sheltered. Nothing had entered me. No drug. No man. Only music. Only death.

And now all I wanted was to let the music out. And to kill in me the dying of my brother. I just wanted to rock.

"Listen, Strobe—" I started.

But he didn't seem to want to listen to me. He got up but motioned for me to stay where I was. He walked around me, where I sat in the middle of the huge loft, the studio off to one side, his home to the other.

As he walked, he talked. "Drugs were my inspiration. I was always looking for some new ways to do things. If I'd done something once, I never wanted to do it again. If I'd played a progression one way, I never wanted to do it that way again. I was using myself up, you know. I mean, how can you go through life without repeating yourself? But I tried. So I got into drugs. *All* kinds of drugs. I ate them, smoked them, sniffed them, shot them up. I took them through my nose, my eyes, my ears, my veins, my hair, my teeth, my gums. I rolled in them, slept in them, sat in them, got on my knees in them and prayed they would never be taken away from me. And they worked! That's the thing about those medicines. They work. I never repeated myself when I was turned on. Everything was new. Fresh. Different. Everything. The love I made. The music I played. There was nothing old, nothing used. I eliminated the past. I re-created myself every day. Until one day . . ."

He stopped. He looked at me. I nodded for him to go on, though I knew what he was going to say. It

30

was Jeffrey all over again. Never wanting to be the same or do the same from one moment to the next. Dying out of his desire to be born anew. The curse of the artist. But it wasn't his story of drugs that I was interested in. It was him. Who was this guy? Where did he come from? Who did he play with? What was his music? Was he real or was I imagining him?

"Until one day I died of an overdose."

Of course! He walked toward me as he said it. So I stood up and started to back away.

He was a ghost. That's what it was. That's what had been bothering me all along. That accounted for the eerie way he looked. He wasn't real. No, he was real, but it was a different reality. He was a dead man. I had auditioned for a dead man. And the only band he was going to play in was a band of angels.

He must have seen that he was scaring me, because he stopped moving. "Not literally, of course."

I wasn't quite sure I believed him.

"My spirit died. Maybe everything I created was new, but it was only novelty. I lived for the future, but I did it by destroying the past. It was all syn-pop. It was electrovision. It was digi-music. It was techno-noise. My keyboard player had a Rhodes electric piano, a Yamaha CP-70 electric grand, a Yamaha MP-1 portable, an E-mu Emulator, and Oberheim OB-Xa and Roland SH-1000 synthesizers. We used to get it all down on a Tascam 38 8-track, Tascam 32 2-track, Studiomaster mixer, Tapco 4400 reverb unit, MXR pitch transposer, Fruman Sound EQ preamp, two PB-

31

64 patch bays, two Yamaha NS-10M monitors, and a couple of Yamaha NS-20T monitors. My drummer was a E-mu Drumulator and some Oberheim digital drums, which gave us eighteen sounds—more than you do, Judy, more than you do." He had droned the names of all the equipment with a computer voice, one pitch and tone.

"So what do you need me for?" I asked.

"Rock and roll," he said. "I want to go back to rock and roll. Enough of this crap." He waved his arms toward the world.

"I just want to rock." I was so tired. I was here in this strange loft with an ex-drug addict who had died, and I was telling him the only truth I knew about myself. I just wanted to rock. I just wanted to rock with some good people.

I expected him to give in. I expected him to put aside his doubts about my sex and my age and my inexperience and to hire me on the spot. I'd put my life in his hands.

But he let me fall through his fingers.

"See you," he said. He was pointing toward the door. Dismissing me.

"When?"

"In the audience, I suppose."

Cold. Cruel.

"I wouldn't pay to see you if you were the last band on earth."

"Neither would I." He put his hand on my shoulder. I didn't know if it was for comfort or to get me out

32

the door. "If it were the last band on earth, I'd want to *be* in it."

"Me too!" I screamed. But it was in my dream that night.

All I said to him in reality was Thank you for your time.

13

What did Strobe do? Did he play lead guitar? Did he sing? Was he the bassist? Keyboardist? Was he a drummer like me, and this was going to be his band with two drummers, like the Allman Brothers or the Dead? All he said was that he ran the band.

What band?

He didn't have a band. He didn't even have a drummer. Only beds. Empty beds. He was alone. Like me. Alone, in that strange loft of his, putting ads in newspapers, the way I put ads in newspapers. We were made for each other. Or at least we were waiting for each other.

But he had sent me away. Why? What kind of test is it to make a drummer play alone? Drummers don't play alone. They circulate the blood. Music is the blood. He said so himself. The body is the band. But there was no music. No band. Only me, playing alone. It wasn't fair. He'd wanted me to fail.

I talked to Jeffrey about it.

Sometimes I did that. I had his ashes. They were in my tom-tom. It had transparent skin, so I could see him, dust inside my music.

Of course, he never talked back. In that way, it was like talking to God. No answer. Except what you found in yourself.

"I don't know what to do. I just want to play in a band. This guy was weird. Weird like you. He's almost from another world. But he knew me. He could tell when my blood was pounding. Like an addict, he said. He was one too. Not just for music. But he's clean now. At least he says he is. He wants to rock. But he doesn't want me. So what am I going to do?"

It was futile to expect an answer, but I shook him anyway. Specks of him flew toward my eyes and washed against the skin of my drum.

"I couldn't tell if he liked my playing. Anyway, drummers don't play alone. I think he wanted me to fail. Even he said it's hard to play solo. So why did he make me? But he wants a drummer. First, I don't think I told him I write songs. Maybe I should send him one of my songs. Maybe what he really needs is music."

I knew I was right. So did Jeffrey. But did he say anything?

That doesn't mean I didn't keep looking down at his ashes when I wrote out for Strobe the song I'd written when Jeffrey had told me there was a girl hidden inside me, and that girl was me:

The Girl Inside the Girl

Everybody wants her,
everybody needs her,
everybody wants to grab a piece
of her life.
But nobody gets her,
and nobody knows her,
and nobody's ever gonna
call her his wife.

'Cause she's the girl,
she's the girl inside the girl,
she's the girl you never find,
not in your heart or in your mind.

Everybody sees her,
everybody hears her,
everybody's hot to know
her phone and her address.
But nobody has her,
and nobody calls her,
and nobody's ever gonna
see her undress.

'Cause she's the girl,
she's the girl inside the girl,
she's the girl you never find,
not in your heart or in your mind.

Everybody loves her,
everybody craves her,
everybody wants to know

how to get her hot.
But nobody makes her,
and nobody takes her,
and only one man is ever
gonna get a shot.

'Cause she's the girl,
she's the girl inside the girl,
she's the girl you never find,
not in your heart or in your mind.

You can give her all your money,
till you're totally broke.
You can christen her with diamonds,
you can sprinkle her with coke.
But you'll never ever have her
and you'll never ever know her
'cause she's the girl,
she's the girl inside the girl.

I mailed it to him.

> STROBE
> 29½ LISPENARD STREET
> 5TH FLOOR
> NEW YORK, N.Y.

I put my name and address on the song and on the envelope. I didn't give him my phone number because I never gave out my phone number except when I had to in my ads.

But of course I waited for him to call anyway. A song is like a love letter. It isn't just supposed to sit there in the world. Something is supposed to *happen*. Passion. Applause. Rejection.

He would never call. He couldn't. But I wanted him to.

Instead, the song was returned by the post office. "Addressee Unknown," written in a very pretty calligraphy, with an arrow shot at my name, "Return to Sender."

How was that possible? Even if his name wasn't Strobe, I had the address, the floor. Why didn't they just leave it there? Why did it come back? None of me was sticking to the outside world.

So I went down to Lispenard Street myself with my song in the envelope. His name was still on the buzzer next to the door, downstairs. That surprised me. Why didn't he get my song?

I rang the bell. Then I backed out into the street and looked up. Come on, key. I closed my eyes and waited for it to fly down and hit me. Let me in. Let me make my music with you. Let me start to live.

It was twilight. Sun from the west tried to bend into these narrow streets. His windows glowed, but I couldn't tell if it was from lights inside or the sun.

"Strobe!" I cried, but it was inside me.

Then I heard my song. Coming down, riding on the sunlight, was my song. He was singing it. All alone. Just his voice. Singing my song.

When he was done, he threw me the key.

15

"I didn't know you wrote," he said.

"I didn't know you sang."

He smiled at me. What a strange face. The skin was so smooth, like a young boy's. But the look in his two-toned eyes was a gaze on eternity.

"It's what I do," he said.

"It sounded good."

"From five flights up." Why was he putting himself down? He seemed so tired. He was tiny in the huge loft, almost thin enough to be part of the still air. And he was dressed all in white.

"That's the point," I said to encourage him. "I could hear you all that way. I could hear every word."

He dismissed that. "You wrote every word."

"Why did you have the post office send it back to me?"

"I didn't. I sent it back myself."

I looked at the envelope. "That's your writing?"

He nodded.

"You mean you wrote 'Addressee Unknown, Return to Sender'?"

He nodded again.

"Why?"

"To let you know how I felt about it."

"So you sent it back to me. Thanks a lot." I was sure he hated it. Was he making fun of it when he sang it? Usually the man's in the street and he sings to his beloved up above. Was this his cruel joke?

"I would have written you a letter. But I couldn't afford a stamp."

I looked around the loft and must have smirked— all that space, that equipment, that independent life.

"Debt," he said. "Old rockers without a band are usually in debt. Even some with bands. Look at Mick Fleetwood. It costs a lot to make music."

"It costs a lot to get high."

Another smile. Better than being asked to leave for my smart-ass remark. "That too," he said.

"So why did you send my song back?"

"I told you. To let you know how I felt about it."

"I get the message. A little late. But I get the message." I started to walk toward the door.

He stopped me. "Did you read what I said?"

"What do you mean?"

He pointed toward the envelope. "Did you open that up?"

"No."

He grabbed it from my hand and tore it open and pulled out my song and handed it to me.

There, at the bottom of the song, in the thinnest, most beautiful handwriting I'd ever seen, just like on the envelope, it said: "This is wonderful. I want to sing your songs. Come back."

I wanted to cry. "Oh," I said. I wanted him to take me in his arms. I wanted to throw myself into them.

He must have read my mind. He turned his back to me and walked away. When you're a winner, you're a loser.

It didn't matter. He wanted my music.

"You can't have my songs without my drums."

"And I won't take your drums without your songs."

"A deal," I said.

"A deal." He motioned for me to come and sit by him on white leather chairs in the middle of the loft. "Now, where are we going to find this band of ours?"

16

He took me everywhere with him. He slid through the night unseen. It was amazing—because he was so distinct. The white hair. The transparent skin. The two-tone eyes. The body like a knife cutting through darkness. But while everyone seemed to notice him, no one saw him. We could go anywhere. We could ask anything and be answered, but we never had to an-

40

swer anything ourselves. No one bothered us. We were ghosts in the machine. I had never been so happy since Jeffrey was alive. I was invisible, with an invisible mystery man. All that was missing was the music we would make together. But we were looking for it. We were looking for our band.

We went to clubs. To concerts. To studios. To Broadway musicals and the opera, where we'd sit way up in the cheapest seats and pass between us a miniature pair of Zeiss binoculars and peer down into the orchestra pit looking for a guitar player and a bass player and a keyboardist, seeing dozens of musicians only by the tiny lights clipped onto their music stands, trying to hear each one of them play out of the sound of the whole orchestra. And we did it, we could hear. We could pick out that one voice as if we were lovers up above being begged to open our arms for a night of ecstasy.

We rarely had to pay to get in anywhere. Everyone seemed to know Strobe, by one name or another. In the clubs, most people called him Strobe. But in concert halls he was Phillip and Zachery and, it was true, Jeffrey, except it was spelled Geoffrey in opera houses, he told me. A girl once called him Sonny, and he turned around to face her and smiled slowly, as if his memory of her met up with her here, now, and I wanted her to die. That was a new feeling for me. I hated it. But I liked where it came from.

He never introduced me. It bothered me at first,

until I realized that it made me feel as if I belonged with him. We were a pair. We were eternal. We went back together to the dawn of time. We needed no introduction.

Sometimes we brought a musician back to Lispenard Street. He'd play. I'd play behind him. Strobe would listen. Then he'd tell the guy to leave.

"What did you think was the matter with him?" I'd ask, if I thought he was good.

"He wasn't better than you," he'd sometimes say when he deigned to say anything.

It was a compliment and a reproach at the same time. A compliment because the musicians we brought home were always very good. A reproach because he was telling me I wasn't good enough not to need someone better to inspire me.

One night, after a bass player had left, sadly hugging his whale to him as he crept off for the long descent to the street, Strobe said to me, "You're improving."

I realized then why he never seemed upset or impatient that we weren't finding musicians for our band. Every time someone came to play with us, and I played with him as he auditioned, I got to practice, and Strobe got to hear me practice, and I was learning how to play with someone else, not just with a record or with my brother singing to me or to the silent music I made inside me. I got to be a drummer in the world, even if Strobe kept telling the world to pack it in and take it somewhere else.

"What are we looking for?" I asked him.

"You'll know it when you hear it."

And of course I did. First Irwin, our keyboardist, and then Maddox, our bassist. And Mark.

17

We found Irwin at Carnegie Recital Hall. It was his New York debut. Like all the other musicians who peeled their first big apple there, he had to pay to rent the hall and then, because no one had ever heard of him, had to give away tickets to get anyone to come. Sometimes a critic from one of the newspapers would show up if there was no one more important to hear that night. But there was always some violinist or cellist or pianist more important playing at Alice Tully Hall or the 92nd Street Y or Merkin Concert Hall or some chamber group at the Metropolitan Museum or some orchestra at Carnegie Hall next door or at Avery Fisher Hall. New York was a musician's heaven and hell. You were never alone and you were always alone.

But even if a critic didn't come, worse critics did, the kind who couldn't judge. Family and friends. They all got free tickets, and they sat there in mortal fear that their son or daughter or best friend or lover would hit a wrong note and New York City would come to a standstill and twenty years of lessons would topple into the sea of debt and shame.

Strobe and I went to recital after recital. We were usually the only ones who hadn't raised the performer or taught him to play or gone to school with him. We were the only ones who heard the music and not the musician.

Irwin came out, and I was expecting the usual rented tuxedo and was prepared to get stabbed in the heart by a memory of Jeffrey. But Irwin was this older guy who was bald on top and had two plates of hair hanging down over his ears, like poor David Crosby when he got put away for drugs and guns, and he wore what must have been his only suit and must have come from the days when he spent time eating instead of practicing, because it hung off him in folds of gray cloth and was almost big enough to cover the enormously wide tie he wore that said "Ft. Lauderdale" from top to bottom. He was also wearing a long scarf around his neck, although it wasn't cold. It reached below the keyboard.

"Uh-oh," said Strobe, who usually said nothing.

If he spoke, I figured I could too. "We should have known," I whispered as Irwin Kolodny bowed. "Look. We're the only people here." Us and the ushers.

"I hadn't noticed," said Strobe. And I believed he hadn't. He sometimes went into a kind of trance before he heard someone play in a place like this. That, or he had a clever way of catching up on his

44

sleep. "Shhh," he hushed me as Irwin's hands rose above the keyboard.

A funny thing happens with music in New York. There is so much of it, and it is so important to the life of the city, the beat of its heart, that it becomes, at night, the city's language. It is spoken everywhere. It is heard by almost everyone. And so, although Strobe and I were the only people who started out at Irwin Kolodny's solo recital and New York debut, by the end of his first piece, a Haydn sonata, about a dozen people had come quietly in; and by the middle of his Schubert impromptu, there were people on either side of us; and when he played the mad first sonata by Robert Schumann, which sounded like a theme song for New York itself, there wasn't a seat to be had in the place and you could hear the held, suffering breath of the audience as it waited to live again for a few minutes in paradise.

Word had spread. That's all. Maybe one or two of the ushers had phoned their friends to get over quick, or had run down into the street to tell the usual musical freaks—who almost lived outside Carnegie Hall and were known to rub their bodies up against it on the Seventh Avenue side—to come into the recital hall if they wanted to hear musical history being made.

But I don't think it was the ushers. I think it was the music. This guy sat down at the piano, he started to play, and the music seeped out through the cracks

45

in the walls and the holes in the ceiling and the air-conditioning ducts, and it was flown out even faster by the waves of pleasure shooting from the brains of me and Strobe as we sat there grooving on the music of this Irwin Kolodny.

New York isn't a city of overnight sensations. It's too impatient for that. When you make it here, you make it before your nails dry.

It was intermission. The place was in an uproar. People couldn't believe their good luck. But there was the usual sadness. The music was so beautiful, but it was so fleeting. The best concerts were like that, a baptism and a funeral.

Then they found a guy with a fancy Walkman hidden in his jacket, the kind that records. They surrounded him. He must have feared for his life when everyone began to reach into their pockets. But it was only to take out their wallets. They shoved money at him along with their business cards, begging him to make copies of his tape for them. Trying to buy their way into musical eternity, to stop the music while they were still alive to hear it.

"We've got to get him," Strobe said. He pulled me out of my seat.

I didn't understand the rush. "It's only intermission."

"We have to get him before he goes back on." Now he pulled me toward the back stairs.

"But he has to finish his recital."

"No he doesn't."

46

"Are you crazy?"

He didn't take it the way I meant it. He stopped and looked at me. "No, I'm not crazy. I've heard enough to know he's our keyboard player. I don't need to hear his Beethoven and his Bartók."

"But what about the rest of his recital?"

Strobe's eyes flashed. "I told you. I don't need to hear it."

I couldn't believe how dense he was. "What do you think, he's giving this recital only for you? He'll stop and ruin his career just because you've heard enough? What are you, the center of the universe?"

"Yes. No. Yes." That's how he answered me before he turned away and dragged me backstage and pulled me over to where Irwin Kolodny was sitting at a table with a cigarette in his mouth and his fingers playing notes on the tabletop.

Strobe watched his hands. "That's not Beethoven, and it's not Bartók," he said.

"So who is it?" said Irwin without looking up.

"Monk."

"What tune?"

" 'Epistrophy.' Monk and Kolodny. *There*." Strobe reached down and put his left hand over Irwin's left hand, stopping the music. "That chord. Pure Kolodny. Just like in the Schumann."

Now Irwin looked at Strobe for the first time. His pinched face opened up, and his flaps of hair seemed about to rise and wave in welcome to the new master.

"You heard that in the Schumann?"

47

"And this one too." Strobe spread out Irwin's fingers on the table in a new configuration.

"So I stuck that minor third in there. I augmented that fifth." Irwin looked away. He was like that new breed of shoplifter called shopputter who puts things into stores instead of taking things out. Inappropriate things. It is a far worse crime than stealing. It upsets the balance.

"You sneaky devil," said Strobe, in his most charming voice. "A little blues."

"A little blues," said Irwin, giggling.

"You want to be in our band?" Strobe asked him.

"I don't know," said Irwin. "I seem to be having something of a triumph here tonight. And I suppose I've been waiting all my life for this," he said guiltily.

Strobe drew closer. Irwin would be breathing Strobe's own sweet breath. "First of all, this is more than something of a triumph. This is a major debut. But if it's going to be *legendary*, then you've got to walk off now. Go back on, Kolodny, and this will be the high point of your life. You know that as well as I do. Is it good enough? Is tonight good enough for that?"

"Feels pretty good to me," said Irwin. I decided I liked this guy.

Strobe looked around. The only other people backstage worked for the place. "You're all alone."

Irwin looked around too. "Yeah. A soloist." He paused. "And my wife left me."

"Why?" I asked. It was like me to do that. I was

48

more into gossip than Strobe, and he was more into mystery.

"Because I never got married." Irwin laughed.

So did Strobe.

I didn't get it. But they did. They laughed. But we were a band, weren't we? Or a band in the making. So they let me in on it.

"Fantasy life," Strobe explained.

"Fantasy life," said Irwin, still laughing.

"Come on, maestro," Strobe said to him. "Let's get out of here."

Irwin played a few more notes on the tabletop. It was his way of thinking.

"You hit a wrong note there," said Strobe.

Irwin broke into the most uproarious laugh I'd ever heard and pushed his way between us and threw his arms around our shoulders and walked us right out the door and through this enormous crowd that was mumbling "Irwin" and "Kolodny" and "Who?"

"Legendary," he said.

He was right.

18

We found Maddox playing electric bass in a gay bar by the piers called Cockles and Muscles where half the men were dressed like cowboys and the other half like accountants and they kept dancing with each other. The cowboys were big and strong. And the accountants were frail. But whenever an accountant told a cowboy to do something—like get a drink or pull out a chair so the accountant could sit down or do kinky things like one by one kissing the tiny holes on the tip of the accountant's shoe—the cowboy did it. You had to figure the accountants all studied karate in their spare time.

Maddox was the only musician backing a singer who I thought was a woman but turned out to be a man, as I discovered to my embarrassment at about four in the morning when (s)he revealed all!

I felt like a jerk. I should have been around long enough by that time to know that for some strange reason there were millions upon millions of human beings who wanted to be the opposite sex. Some of them even changed instruments in the middle of life's symphony, so to speak.

The singer's name was Hortense (don't ask me why). She didn't have a bad voice for either a woman or a man; it was that kind of smoky cabaret style like Marlene Dietrich where everything is a seduction.

Hortense would sing for ten minutes and disappear for half an hour and then come back in some new girlish outfit and sing for another ten minutes. They all loved her. They applauded when she came out and applauded when she left. (Maybe they knew what was going to happen at four A.M. and were encouraging her to stick around.) But what only Strobe and I seemed to know was that what made Hortense great was not her voice and not her outrageous costume changes and not the promise of seeing her change from a woman to a man with one flick of her Bic.

What made Hortense great was her one and only accompanist, who moved between electric bass and concert acoustic bass and the smaller piccolo bass like Ron Carter's, depending on what song Hortense was singing, and gave her almost all the coloring necessary for this sensitive kind of singing. Hortense didn't have a bad voice, but Maddox made it into a great voice by supporting it from below or extending its range above.

"I can't believe what I'm hearing," said Strobe after we'd been there for two of Hortense's sets.

"You don't know which one is singing," I said.

Strobe looked at me as if I were his prize pupil. It made me want to kiss him and kick him.

Strobe was not unknown in this place. We were left pretty much alone at our table, but once in a while someone would come up to us—or to him, actually—and ask what was happening, and Strobe would say he was putting together a band, and I was his drummer, and the person would look at me, and a number of them then whispered something to Strobe, and Strobe would say, "A girl," and the same number of them would lose interest in me.

They all called Strobe Danny in this place. It didn't surprise me anymore to find he had yet another name.

"Are you gay too?" I asked him.

"I'm not gay. I'm not straight. I gave all that up a long time ago. In another life. My flesh is mine—what's left of it. I don't share."

Somehow, that made me more comfortable with Strobe. There would be no men in his life. No women in his life. Just me. Just us. Just the band.

But he was so strange. He was strange the way Jeffrey had been strange. Except he was stronger. Jeffrey had died. Strobe had come back from death.

Strobe got one of the bartenders to come over and take a note to Maddox on stage. Maddox read the note and came over and sat down. No one said anything. He looked around as if he'd just arrived and hadn't seen it all from the stage. (I was yet to learn that you don't see much of anything from most stages.)

"Doesn't say much for the Marlboro man, this place," he said.

"Then why do you play it?" Strobe asked.

"It's work." Spoken like a true musician.

"Come work with us."

"Who's us?" Maddox was one of those proud black guys. Disdainful. You figured he'd look down his nose at the sky.

"This is Judy Valentine. She's our drummer. Irwin Kolodny is—"

"This little chick is your drummer?" Maddox leaned close to me across the small round table pitted with the names of gay men who had taken the time to carve one night of their lives into Cockles and Muscles.

He reached out and grabbed both my arms.

"Get your hands off me!"

He squeezed my arms.

"Muscles," he said, letting go. "Let me see your hands."

I made fists.

Maddox looked at Strobe. Strobe looked at me.

I opened my fists.

Maddox took my hands in his hands and rubbed his palms over my calluses.

He liked what he felt. A hard girl was good to find.

Then I grabbed his hands and turned them over and ran my fingertips over his. His calluses made mine feel like mushrooms. They were like parts of his instrument. Mine were just parts of my sticks.

But he had liked what he felt.

"Who else is us?" he said.

"Irwin Kolodny on keyboards."

"That cat who walked out on Carnegie Hall?"

"That cat."

"An honor." Maddox leaned back now. He seemed to trust us. Then his eyes blazed into Strobe. "And you, my man?"

Strobe ignored him. "All we're missing now is lead guitar."

"Guitar, bass, keyboards, drums," Maddox went over the band. "Who are *you*, McNamara?"

Strobe nodded. He liked this insolent Maddox guy. He raised his arms and made like a conductor. The three of us sang together, "Oh, my name is McNamara, I'm the leader of the band. . . ."

"So?" Maddox wasn't going to let Strobe off the hook.

"Vocals," said Strobe.

"Can you sing?"

"You want to feel my tongue?" Strobe stuck it out toward Maddox. It perched there above the middle of the table like a questionable fish. Maddox pointed at it and opened his eyes wide. I broke up. Strobe let it swim back into his mouth.

"Whose tunes?"

"Mine. Hers."

"Lyrics?"

"She writes those too."

"Does she know enough?" Maddox asked about me.

"About what?" I asked back.

"Life," said Maddox.

"No," I answered. "That's why I write such good songs."

Maddox looked at me like he'd found his long-lost sister.

"Rock and roll?" he asked, and the words set the fingers of his right hand to twitching.

"Rock and roll," we told him.

"When do we rehearse?" he said, which was also a polite way of asking when he'd get to hear us play.

For all he knew, we couldn't play taps on Judgment Day.

"When we find our guitar player for Judy," Strobe answered.

I thought it was just a figure of speech. I toasted them with my Tab.

19

We found my guitar player in Central Park.

He wasn't bunched up with all the other musicians, who stretched from the east side to the west side along the 72nd Street transverse: steel bands and bagpipers and flute-playing girls and always a couple of old black guys with a harmonica and a guitar singing songs like "That woman of mine was a hard luck charm,/First she raked my body, then she raked my farm."

Mark The Music was in the middle of the Great Lawn, playing solo to the whole city on a tiny amp. When you looked up from that place, and you turned around, New York was a flying ship of domes and pinnacles, blinking and twitching; or the balcony of a great hall, explosive with adoration.

No one was listening to him. He was alone in the middle of that great green space, playing fantastic bluesy licks that bent the trees.

His guitar case was closed; that meant he was either rich or stupid.

Strobe threw a dollar on it anyway (he must have *really* liked this guy). The bill just lay there. The musician gave Strobe a kind of disgusted look.

He was a goofy-looking boy. He was dressed all in black, in an old tuxedo, except for red suspenders and high, brown, cracked leather boots that he wore outside his pants and that gave him the look of a hip woodsman. On his head was a black top hat that had MARK THE MUSIC printed on it in red.

He was all smiles. Even his disgusted look was a smile.

"Do you like him?" Strobe asked me.

"Great chops," I said, hoping the guy couldn't hear me.

"Do you like him?"

I knew what Strobe was getting at. Teasing me. Fixing me up. What was the matter with men? They never meant it. Usually they wanted you for themselves. But they always pushed other guys on you, just for the pleasure of watching you turn them down.

"Not to marry," I answered.

That didn't get a rise out of Strobe. "Do you want him?"

"He plays great guitar."

Strobe looked over at him. "Take the money," he said.

The boy looked down at the bill sitting on his guitar case, removed both hands from his beat-up old Tele-caster for a moment, then put both hands back on and said, "Go, Shakespeare," and played a riff that took that dollar bill and sent it flying into the air and heading out over the Great Lawn until a group of kids saw it and started to chase it, and this incredible musician seemed to make it rise and fall at the will of his guitar, leading the kids on like the Pied Piper of Manhattan down Electric Avenue.

"Wow!"

He stopped playing and bowed toward me.

"Who's Shakespeare?" Strobe asked him.

"My guitar," he answered.

"This is Judy," Strobe said.

"Mark The Music," he said to me.

"I did," I said. "You're great."

"That's my name as well." His voice was soft and formal. I got the impression he used it sparingly, like a lot of musicians.

"What is?"

"Mark The Music."

"Your last name is Music?" Strobe asked.

"And his middle name is The!" I said.

"Like?" he asked me.

"Like Winnie The Pooh!" I answered.

He almost jumped up and down with glee. "I'll be in your band," he said.

"How did you know—?"

"Do you know how many bands there are?" he interrupted me. "Do you know how many people come up to me here and ask me to be in their band?"

"How many?"

"None. I'm too good."

"Then how did you know—?"

"It's always been my fantasy. I stand here playing my guitar, and someone comes up to me and asks me to be in their band. Isn't that everybody's fantasy? You stand there doing something and someone comes up and asks you to do it with them?"

"To play in their band," I said.

"To play in their band."

Now we were a band.

A bald keyboard player who had become famous for walking out on fame and fortune for the sake of rock and roll.

A black bass player who carried the same name as the former governor of Mississippi who had attacked black people with an ax handle.

A teenage guitar player who could do magic with music and was a ghost come to haunt me and to love me.

A singer who was the second greatest mystery in my life.

A girl drummer, who was the greatest mystery.

I was in the arms of my band. From out of nowhere, hidden, in the back, unseen, I reached forth and powered our music. My arms reached out into the world and beat our blood from our heart into its heart.

And I hid in the arms of my band, as I had always dreamed of doing. They surrounded me like a family of sound. They hid me from the world. No matter how famous I might get, I knew I could remain unknown.

20

We rehearsed at Strobe's place on Lispenard Street. Once we found Mark and were a full band, we met there the next day. No one had much to say to anyone else. Musicians don't talk all that much. Or at least not until they feel comfortable. And they usually don't feel comfortable unless they're playing, not talking.

It was a strange gathering. Only Strobe and I had heard the others play. We had come together like stray atoms in the universe. What were we going to make when life glued us all together?

Strobe reminded us of our heritage.

"We have to rock," he said. "Rock is life. I need that music. I was headed for the graveyard. I died and came back. That's what music's for. Life. We are life. Picture what happens before that stage. Thousands of hands reach out to touch you. Girls scream and faint. Boys want to be you. To *be* you. Can you imagine what it takes to make someone want to be you? They will give up their lives for yours. And not only that"—Strobe stopped for a second and gave us a smile that was, I admit, a relief after his preaching that had my hair standing on end—"but they will wear your face on their T-shirts!" He laughed. "You will see yourself all over the world on the chests of people who love us."

I believed him. I knew what he said was true. When you rocked, life changed around you. And it was all in my hands: It was the drummer who gave life to music.

Maddox wasn't buying Strobe's jive, though. "Hey, man," he said, "what is it exactly you *do*?"

"I told you. Vocals."

"Anyone ever heard him sing?"

"I have," I said.

"Where?"

"In the street."

"He sang to you in the street?"

"I was in the street. He was up here."

Maddox scoffed. "Romeo and Juliet! Has anyone ever heard him sing with a band? I mean, who are you, man?"

"Let's do it!" said Strobe.

He gave us all music. I thought the piece would be a mystery. But it wasn't. I had written it. Strobe was collecting all my songs.

We got into place, with our instruments, and Strobe pointed to Irwin, who opened the piece. And to me, who was always there.

We started to play.

And Strobe started to sing.

Alone (Alone Again)

I have seen you, walking through the night,
invisible, to the naked eye.
I have known you, in the dark that knows no
*   light,*
you let our love die, you let our love die.

I have held you, lying on my bed,
and listened to you lie.
I've believed every heartfelt word you said,
you let our love die, you let our love die.

Alone, alone again,
I don't like women and I'm through with men.
Don't know what I ever saw in you,
You never made me laugh, you never made me
*   new.*

I have heard you, telling all your lies,
silent, in your endless eyes.
I have watched you, on the inside of my head,
you killed our love, you killed our love dead.

I have touched you in the middle of my sleep
and held you on my thigh.
I have let you into the deepest of my deep,
you let our love die, you let our love die.

Alone, alone again,
I don't like women and I'm through with men.
Don't know what I ever saw in you,
Ha ha, tell me, lover, now what're you gonna do?

Who could have known how he could sing? I'm the only one who'd heard him, and that was in the street, Romeo and Juliet, his voice wrapped in wind. But now he sang for the band, as if no one were there or else everyone were there, the entire population of the world, hanging on every word, watching his every move, the hairs on his head, his wet lips, the glint of his teeth, his struggling hands.

He was transformed when he sang. He sang with his whole body. And out of it came a voice that made the rest of us look at one another. Who is this man? Where does that voice come from? How can such perfect sound come from a human being?

He entered your body when he sang to you.

And we all gave ourselves up to him. Irwin and Maddox and Mark and I. We lay down low and let him have his way with us.

With his voice, he married us all.

21

We named the band after our marriage: Wedding Night. It was a name that promised a hot evening. A once-in-a-lifetime experience. It would have been a lousy name for a normal band: all guys. It was a great name for a band of boys and a girl. I was the mystery bride.

Strobe wanted me to dress in white. But I dressed

in black, the way I always had. Backdrops were dark. I liked to blend into them. I wished my skin were darker too. Then all anyone would have seen were my drumsticks, moving so fast they made fans out of thin air, fans of light and fans of sound.

At first we were playing dumps. We were a loft band, a bar band, a lounge band, a pit band with no hovering stage, just a pit, all around us. We played in places with names like Shake a Leg, the Lie-Ins Club, Clean Teen, and the Brassiere. And those were only the ones in New Jersey.

Irwin had a van. He had always had a van. Here was this lonely man who had spent his whole life practicing the piano, and he never got married and he bragged that he never even had a date—and for years he had owned a van that had rattled around empty behind him and he used to dream, he told us, that it would be filled with kids, and he would be taking them ice-skating.

So we bounced around in Irwin's van. I took up the most space, not with my body, which was the smallest, but with my drums. No one commented on this. It has been so in bands since the dawn of time.

22

We were "discovered" one night in our first fancy downtown club, called Adrenaline. If you didn't know

63

where the place was, you wouldn't be able to find it. It was like Area used to be: a metal door stuck like a bandage on a shabby building.

After midnight the whole world would congregate on that unlikely street, empty except for the limos and cabs and motorcycles that would pull up, and suddenly Adrenaline would be inhabited by the most outrageously wonderful people in costumes and evening dress, undershirts and leather and studs, and they would crowd onto the small dance floor and mingle their feathers and their metal and, as Jeffrey used to call it, their deeply polished flesh, and worship the band by dancing to its music.

These clubs never lasted very long. Usually, the people in the front lines of life, the discoverers of new worlds, would get bored with their alternate planets and disappear overnight, like migrating birds, and the club would fold within a week. But sometimes the young and the dirty from the other boroughs would arrive, and bribe the door whores, and pretty soon they would take over in hordes, plopping down their six dollars a drink because they were ashamed not to and turning the dance floor into a gym. The owners got rich when this happened; but their clubs got ruined.

So no matter which way a club went—into the oblivion of bankruptcy or the oblivion of popularity—it really lived for only a few months, when everyone in the world felt they had to be there even though they didn't know where it was or what it was or how it was or even what it was called. All they knew was that they needed to be part of its history so it could be part of theirs.

Adrenaline used recorded music and videos like all the other clubs. But it had grown famous for its live acts. We were opening for the featured band, which was called Mucous Membrane. We were just there to add some flesh to the videos and to loosen up the crowd, like one of those strange comics who has to make a studio audience laugh before the taping of a TV comedy show.

"It's when the second fiddle comes first," said Strobe. He wasn't happy about opening for anyone.

"Second fiddle," said Irwin, starting to think. His fingers went up into his hair. He looked like the mad professor. "Such a downer. 'Second fiddle.' Look what it's come to mean. And the truth of it is that the second fiddle often carries the first. Beethoven wrote parts for the second fiddle that—"

"Stick to the subject," said Maddox.

"What is the subject?" asked Kolodny.

"This gig."

"I'm up for it," said Mark The Music, playing the dead strings on his unamplified guitar as we waited to go on. Just in the rhythm of choked sounds I could hear what tunes he was playing. They were all mine.

Nothing much else was happening. We were just hanging out. You didn't horse around before you went on. You didn't drink or dope or otherwise mess around. Music was serious business. Ours in particular.

Wedding Night was a tight band. We were rehearsed just to the edge of anxiety, where you're sick of the tunes for yourselves and the only way to get happy is to play them in public. A band needs to feel part of the world, just the way I needed to feel part of a band.

And this band was on the verge of jumping off the edge of the world.

23

"LADIES AND GENTLEMEN, PLEASE GET YOUR ADRENA-LINE FLOWING FOR . . . WEDDING NIGHT!"

We were on the stage when the lights went up. No flashy entrances for us. After all, it's hard to cause a commotion by coming on one at a time when no one knows who you are in the first place.

So it was just white light . . . and there was Wedding Night.

We opened with a piece of bravado that Strobe had written called "A Hard Place," which was a very sexy little number about a guy who gets up for rock and roll. Naturally, he was "between rock and a hard place" too. I mean, the lyrics were pretty dumb. But it was a great song to use to test out an audience, because we drowned out the words with this incredible rising tide of open sound, wave after wave of Mark's guitar rippling notes in a way that I had suggested to him when I played him an old tape Jeffrey had made of John Coltrane on his tenor saxophone and told him what Jeffrey had said about Coltrane's creating sheets of sound.

Everyone got to solo in this first piece, except me (I didn't believe in drum solos). All I did was sit back there behind what Strobe called the Berlin Wall of my drums and, hidden from view, drive my boys home.

How can I say what it felt like? There is nothing in the world—now that I have tried everything, or at least everything that I want to try—that is as joyous as playing the drums in a great rock and roll band. You are life itself. *Boom boom boom.* You get to wear the Drummer's Smile. You and only you.

The guys would look back at me. They could just about see my face. But I knew it was all lit up. It must have been like looking at a baby's face. One look at me, and they beamed. I was starting to sweat already, so I shook my head and watched the beads of water fly off and turn color as the light man upstairs went a little nuts at the end of the tune.

There wasn't much applause. There never is at clubs. People come to dance. Between dances, when the band is live, they get a chance to talk, which is impossible when a DJ is playing records and runs one song into another to try to banish silence and loneliness and to let perfect strangers dance and touch and never have to lock eyes or say a word. But with us, they got a chance to drink and to say "Mmmmmmmm." That's all we could hear up there. "Mmmmmmmm." But we knew what they were saying. We knew they liked us. Because they didn't really stop dancing when we stopped playing. Their feet were moving, their hips, their shoulders, their great, great asses, moving, prancing, shaking, dancing. We got their murmur of approval. And that's when we really gave ourselves to them.

24

The funny thing is, there's always a letdown when you finish. Even if you're so tired you don't think you can swing a stick above your waist or lower your toes against your bass, you get afraid of finishing. You get so much into the music when you're playing it, you're afraid that when you stop, and the sound dies, slowly ringing in your ears, you'll die too.

So I was feeling kind of sad when we walked off after doing the eight numbers they told us we could do before they broke for records and prepared the setup for Mucous Membrane. Strobe held me up on one side, Mark The Music on the other, and they walked me off like teammate buddies. Maybe they could tell I had postpartum depression.

"How'd it go?" I asked.

"Fabulous!" said Mark. He looked like he wanted to hug me.

"I need more songs from you" was all that Strobe said.

"I don't have any more songs."

"You're one big song, Judy. Just cut a few more pieces off yourself."

It sounded so cruel. I let go of Strobe and let Mark bear the burden of the weary girl drummer.

"Have fun, you two," Strobe said. He walked away, between Irwin and Maddox, who had formed the natural bond of bassman and keyboardist and knew more about music than any of us, except Mark was the best musician, Mark was magic. Sometimes he held Shakespeare to him with the neck at his body and the body in the middle of his body, and he closed himself around it, and made it disappear, and you swore he was playing himself and his flesh rang with the violent, beautiful sounds he tore from it. Mark was magic.

But Strobe was the magician. He had split us all down the middle. Two plus two. That way he could walk unscathed between us, and when he wanted us, he drew us in from the side. And when he didn't want us, he sent us off to play. Just like now.

25

"Want a beer?" Mark asked me.

"We're too young to drink," I said.

"They always serve the band. You can be twelve years old, and they'll serve you."

"All right," I said. "Make mine a Tabweiser."

He started off, did a double take, and then looked back at me, laughing. He was such a cute kid, Mark The Music. He had dark soft hair that fell nearly over his eyes and eyes like fat black olives and a wide mouth that twisted up to one side when he smiled, like now, making his pretty face just a little dumb-looking, or maybe not dumb but quizzical. I didn't like pretty boys anyway. Lucky for Mark he was usually smiling so his real beauty showed through.

He pulled me ahead by the arm. There seemed to be a lot of people around us all of a sudden. "We have to go to the private bar," he said. "A beer'll cost us five bucks or something at the folks' bar."

"How do you know there's a private bar?"

"There's always a private bar."

But we couldn't move. We were surrounded. By fans!

You were great, they said. Far out, they said. Too much, they said. Outasight, they said. Great band, they said.

Thank you, thank you, thank you, thank you.

I was in a strange head. It was as if they were talking about somebody else. I couldn't relate the praise to me. I just wanted to hide from it. I was filled with an overwhelming desire to get behind my drums and power forth.

Not Mark. He ate it up.

70

"And where did you get your name?" someone asked him. " 'Mark The Music.' Where did you get such a name as that?" He had a pencil poised, waiting for the answer.

"Are you a reporter?" Mark asked.

"As it happens."

"I still can't tell you."

"Is it your given name?"

"It's my taken name."

The reporter laughed and wrote that down. "Good quote. That's good enough for me. Thanks for your time." And then the man held out his hand. He wanted Mark to shake it. He wanted Mark to *touch* him. He wanted the feel of a rising star against his skin.

Mark shook his hand like the good boy he was. "Where you from?" he asked. "*New York Times, Rolling Stone?*"

"*Foxy,*" said the reporter.

"Who, me?" asked Mark, looking confused.

"No," said the man. "I mean, yes. But *Foxy* is the name of my publication. You've never heard of it? *Foxy?*"

"*Foxy?*" Mark was incredulous.

"It's read by over a hundred thousand teenage girls," said the reporter.

"Gimme a beer!" Mark grabbed my hand and pulled me away as if all those girls were in pursuit and I was the only one he wanted.

26

There was a private bar. Not only that. There was a private *everything*.

Off down a long corridor, which seemed to be guarded at the beginning and end by men whose clothes-bursting bodies had been created by bicycle pumps, and whose necks were as wide as their shoulders, was a huge room filled with music and smoke and home movies and liquor and pills and remarkable haberdashery and people who came in all the colors of the human rainbow.

"Oh, boy!" said Mark. "What'd I tell you?"

"Who are all these people?"

As if I had called forth a genie with my very question, an older man in a gray double-breasted suit with a tie the color of a raspberry whispered in my ear, "Welcome to the playpen of the privileged."

"Who are you?"

Not quite answering my question, Mark said to the man, "Hey, I know you."

"How kind of you to say so." The man held out his hand.

Mark took it. "I mean, I recognize you. I've seen your picture a million times. I just . . ."

"I know," the man said kindly. "You know me.

You've seen me. You've heard of me. I'm famous. It's just my name that escapes you."

"How did you know?" asked Mark.

I laughed at his innocence.

"From that expression on your face. The same one that Ms. Valentine just reacted to so affectionately."

Did I blush? Not me. Never. But I went through all the motions. In other words, the heat rose, but the color stayed the same.

"My name is Edgar Lieberman. I'm—"

"Argh!" Mark groaned in embarrassed elation.

"—the president of Entity Records."

"I know, I know," breathed Mark.

"Judy Valentine," I said unnecessarily, but they were the only two words I remembered at the moment.

"Don't get all excited," said Mr. Lieberman. "I'm only a businessman, first of all. I just make deals, I make money, I go home and count my money, and I wake up with a funny taste in my mouth just like everybody else. And second, I'm not going to tell you how wonderful you were tonight and offer you a recording contract."

"You're not?" Mark seemed crestfallen.

"This is not a book or a movie," said Mr. Lieberman. "Real life doesn't work like that."

"Mine does," said Mark.

"How so?"

"I was standing there one day in Central Park thinking that it was going to be the last day of my life unless somebody came up to me and asked me to be in their band, and somebody did. She did. And he did." Mark must have known Strobe was somewhere in the room. "They saved my life. And they gave me a new one. I was rescued at the last moment. Just like in a movie. Just like in real life."

I believed him. And I realized at that moment that Jeffrey must have been the same. Here today, gone . . . today. Nothing to it. No big deal. Nothing to get hung about. And I wanted to hold him to me forever, Mark, hold him like a brother.

Mr. Lieberman didn't seem at all perplexed by Mark's announcement. He simply said, "Then it's everyone's good fortune that you found each other. And I take back what I said before. Real life *does* work like that. It must. Ergo, you *will* have a recording contract with Entity Records."

We did invisible cartwheels, Mark and I, and came to rest only when our master's serious voice split the heavens with cruel good sense: "On what terms?"

"Ah, Strobe," said Mr. Lieberman.

"Hello, Edgar," said Strobe.

They knew each other from Strobe's previous life.

"You've finally put together a great band."

Strobe nodded cautiously.

"Great musicians," Mr. Lieberman went on.

Strobe kept nodding.

"Only one problem."

Strobe stopped nodding.

"You need better material, Strobe. There were only

three good songs tonight. Three out of twelve. Do you know what that would mean for an album? Three out of twelve? They'd be selling that album at Tower Records out of bins for twenty-nine cents before you'd even returned from your supporting tour. I'll give you a recording contract. And on *my* terms. But I won't release a record until you get some better tunes. So far I've heard only three."

"Which three?"

Mr. Lieberman named them. He even went back to being nice Mr. Lieberman and sang some of them. They were mine.

"Those are hers," said Strobe.

Mr. Lieberman looked at me as if it were the Second Coming and who should show up to save the world but a girl drummer.

27

We closed down Adrenaline that night. That morning.

At about six thirty in the A.M. the five of us staggered out of there, our arms somewhere around one another. Strobe was in the middle. He pulled us all together up toward Fourteenth Street, as if his arms were a fence around us. The rest of us talked.

We talked about the club and the other band, Mucous Membrane, which had lived up to its name so that people began to wave white handkerchiefs at them in surrender. And it was to us they had surrendered. They were the kind of band that had guitars shaped like lightning bolts and transparent drums with live rodents inside them that went crazy with the noise and eventually died and a drummer who held his sticks in artificial hands though his own were perfectly good and a synthesist so dominant that he reproduced everyone else's sounds, drowning them out completely, and was also the lead vocalist and fed his singing through his machine so he came out sounding like a man trapped in the organ at Our Lady of the Parakeet Church way uptown.

Mucous Membrane was waved off and Wedding Night was called back on. We blew the place apart. I could tell, though I could hear nothing from the floor. Our own music veiled us from the uproar and the adulation.

But later, back in the private suite, I saw a video of us. I'd never seen myself play before. Or the band.

Maddox was like a black tree, standing there, hardly moving his feet, turning on his hips, now toward Mark, now toward Irwin, smiling at Irwin, only shaking his head at Mark, the way you do when you don't believe what you're seeing or hearing or tasting or knowing. That Mark was magic.

Irwin bounced on his beloved round piano stool and swiveled between instruments. His scarf blew in the wind he made. He occasionally threw in little classical riffs, as if to tell us he was slumming. When I saw his face on the screen, I knew that wherever he'd moved to the slum from, it was Retirement Village now for him. This guy had gone fishin'. This mad professor just got tenure. He was *home*.

Mark was a star. You could tell the minute you saw him on the screen. He was our pretty boy. And so innocent. His wide-open eyes made Paul McCartney's look like paper cuts. He was going to have girls coming after him in numbers to dwarf the falling leaves of autumn.

Strobe was mesmerizing. Who did he remind me of? Rod Stewart? Sting? Meat Loaf? Prince? He was everybody. Nobody. You couldn't grasp him, and so you just stared at him. I watched him on the screen as if I had never seen him or met him in my life. He was someone else. He was transformed.

All you could see of me was the top of my head. It was a flying saucer, moving to the beat. Once in a while I raised a stick and you saw it bullet through the air, the color of whatever light they were trying to dye me at that moment. I remained impervious. I powered that band from behind. I was the unseen force. I liked it that way. If I could have been completely invisible, I would have been. There was freedom.

Wedding Night had its wedding night that night. Double duty. We rose from the dead of our first set and were carried out on the shoulders of our second. They loved us.

Then they forgot about us. Music came lasering on down from the DJ, and the moment our adoring audience began to dance to the gurgle and burping of "Paint a Rumour," we were a memory buried one music layer lower in their minds. We were gone. Until later. When my tunes would rise in their morning sleep and be the sound track for their dreams.

"Where do we go from here?" asked Mark to all of us as we continued uptown.

"We cut a record," said Maddox.

"We tour," said Kolodny.

"Where we go from here is the Empire Diner," said Strobe authoritatively, brooking no dissent. He was the boss. But everyone was correct.

28

Strangely, it was that *Foxy* reporter who gave us our first notice. He must have been a stringer for the *Post*, because in Friday's weekend edition there was an unsigned piece that could have been written only by him. Headlined WEDDING NIGHT PUMPS ADRENALINE, it went on to say that we had saved the club from sure destruction by coming on again after Mucous Membrane was trashed—our return to the basics of rock and roll was a revolution in itself these days of bands put together for the looks of their boys and the electronic complexity of their machines—we were on the verge of signing with Entity—our lead singer seemed like a mysterious spirit-being from another world, so distant was he, until he sang and his voice seemed to rise from the very earth beneath the city, all gravel and fire and wind—our guitarist, whose strange name, Mark The Music, was not a given name but a taken one, combined the flash of Jimmy Page with the finesse of Mark Knopfler—our drummer was a little slip of a girl who hid away behind her drums as if to tease people into thinking that only a giant could produce so tempestuous a rhythm and so enveloping a sound, and when she stood up and left her drums and joined the rest of the band for its bows, a buzz went up and amazement and then desire rushed through the audience, which realized that its atavistic fear of the power of her drumming was replaced by a protective love for her small, semigloved hands and her delicate body. . . .

The guys made fun of me. In the middle of our rehearsing some of my new songs at Strobe's, when I was in the middle of pushing Mark through the bridge on "Your Place or Mine?" he stopped playing and bent over and I thought he was having a heart attack. I jumped over my drums and swooped down on him from behind and put my arms around him and raised him slowly up and, expecting to find the face of death again in my life, found him pink with sucking in his laughter, which came out carrying his "Oh, forgive me, forgive me, I am suffering from my atavistic fear of your drumming."

And everyone broke up. Except Strobe. Who let us

79

all get in our jollies before he made us get back to work.

"We're on the verge of destruction," he said.

"Hey, man, we're on the verge of *success*," said Maddox.

"That's what I mean." Strobe liked to play philosopher. He must have figured he earned it by coming back from the dead. "We're hot. I can feel it. But we haven't done anything yet. One successful gig after months in the toilets of New Jersey. This is when success and failure meet. When you're on the verge of anything, you're also on the verge of what you're leaving behind. And what we're leaving behind is failure. If—"

"Right on," said Maddox sarcastically. Sometimes Maddox thought Strobe was too much jive.

Strobe gave him an icy look. "If we get anywhere," he finished.

"To the top," said Irwin. "I didn't give up a career in the salons of North America in order to miss playing in its stadia."

" 'Stadia!' " Mark repeated. " 'Stadia!' " He bent over again.

"The plural of *stadium*," Irwin explained.

It was more than Mark could bear. "I am suffering from my atavistic fear of stadia," he stammered before he washed us once again with his laughter.

"Enough," Strobe said finally. And he whipped us on.

So much was happening so quickly.

29

Strobe showed up one night with a business manager. His name was Mitch Sunday. He listened to us rehearse for a while and then sat us down.

He didn't look like a businessman to me. For one thing, he was probably still in his twenties, and even if I was only sixteen, twenty-nine didn't seem all that old when it came to running our careers. I would have preferred to cast my fate with an older man in a gray suit with a hard face and eyes that flashed like diamonds.

Mitch Sunday, on the other hand, dressed New York laid-back, which meant he wore pleated black pants, a loose gray shirt buttoned all the way up to his neck, and ankle-top shoes with shallow-cleated Vibram soles. He was a little overweight. Maybe it went with the territory. And he kept playing with his hair. Maybe he was proud of it.

Mitch talked like someone who went to Coney Island Business School. Step right up, ladies and gentlemen. . . .

"You guys are on the verge of really busting out. You got most of what it takes. You got a great name. Wedding Night. Real good, real good. It's clean. It's dirty. It's white. It's black. The main thing is, it really speaks to your audience. And do you know what it tells them?"

I was tempted to raise my hand. But I had no idea what it told them. Who were they anyway?

"It tells them, tonight's the night. That's what it tells them. Tonight's the night." He began to sing Rod Stewart's "Tonight's the Night." He didn't have a bad voice, actually. Then Mark started to sing Neil Young's "Tonight's the Night."

Pretty soon it was a duel, with Mitch singing of love and sex and Mark singing of drugs and death. They were trying to drown out one another.

Finally Mitch stopped and said, "Stick to your guitar, kid. Stick to your genius."

Mark looked hurt. Not that he ever sang with us. Only Strobe sang for Wedding Night. But maybe Mark The Music had fostered dreams of becoming the ultimate in macho rock: the lead guitarist who sings lead. Even Pete Townsend didn't do that.

"As I was saying," said Mitch, "you've got the name. And you've got the personnel. Solid musicians in the back. Irwin here, for the old hippies. Maddox for the funk. He may not be Michael Jackson, but—"

Maddox gave Mitch a look that only a black guy can give a white guy. Mitch's words froze in their tracks.

Then Mitch tipped his hat to Maddox. It was a gesture of reconciliation. Never mind that Mitch didn't have a hat.

"Mark here has a weird name, which is only to the good, he's cute as a Menudo, he dresses like someone running a circus, he can play the guitar as fast and as clean as anyone I ever heard. He's got the power chords too. But his metal is just heavy enough. I know what you people are up to. One step back, two steps ahead. Right? Right. The best of the past and the better of tomorrow. None of this hands-off rock and roll, none of this telephone pop, none of this Pacman poopoo. But you ain't Blue Oyster Cult either. You ain't Led Zeppelin or Whitesnake or *Pyromania.* What you guys are is . . ."

He was right not to say. I think he would have been fired on the spot if he tried to stick us in someone else's *hole de pigeon*, as Jeffrey used to say.

"Strobe is . . . Strobe is . . . Strobe is . . . Well, to tell you the truth, boys and girls, I don't know what Strobe is. Strobe is *it.* Strobe is the great mystery at the heart of Wedding Night. Strobe is *droit du seigneur*, if you know what I mean. Strobe has the greatest voice and the greatest stage presence in rock and roll today." He looked at Strobe, who looked back at him with undisguised bewilderment. Who needed a business manager who told you how great you are? He was supposed to tell other people how great you are. What was this, a rehearsal? Then Mitch went on. His voice became different now. He sounded like an accountant instead of a barker. "But Strobe is never going to be loved. Be that as it may. You don't love God, do you? When it comes to God, you tiptoe. You whisper. But man, can He sing! And man, does He sell records!"

83

Mitch was back to his old self. "And your drummer. This girl. What are we going to do with this girl? She *hides*. Do you know that? You probably don't because she's behind you. But do you know what she does while she's behind you? She hides. It's like two hands playing the drums. That's all you can see of her. And let's face it, a girl drummer is a rarity these days. Even in an all-girl band, a girl drummer is a rarity. But in the kind of band you've got here, in this quintessential rock band that is like a natural element driving forth with the power of the wind, a girl drummer is unheard of. But she shouldn't be unseen. This is not a gimmick, this girl. This is not a hoax. This is not a novelty. This girl can play the drums like . . . I mean, it is lucky that Bonzo and Moonie are dead already. That's all I have to say about it. And her songs. . . . How can a little teenager like this write songs like that? Who is she? Where does she come from?"

He stopped and looked around at us. He was leaning forward. Veins stood out in his forehead. His eyes were mouths. His hands were his ax. He was obviously the business manager par excellence. We would have paid to hear ourselves at that point.

"Don't you get what I'm saying?" he pleaded. "Don't you understand? This girl is your main attraction. Without her, you are five fine musicians. With her, you are a band."

I wanted to disappear.

"And I'm going to make you the biggest band in the world."

30

We were a long way from that. We were just a group of musicians who had a sound and songs of our own and had played in a few New Jersey and Pennsylvania and Delaware dives and at state universities in what seemed like sixty states but was really only seven and for one night had surfaced above the murk of endless pop music to become the hot band that almost no one had ever heard.

Mitch Sunday was going to make us the biggest band in the world. What a huck! And what was amazing was how fast it happened.

Strobe took me aside after Mitch had left and told me that Mitch was right. I was the main attraction.

"I don't want to be that," I said.

"Let me make you some tea." He went toward the kitchen. "Everybody out," he said to the others. "Back here tomorrow at noon. Maybe we'll have some new tunes."

Maddox put on his new leather jacket. Kolodny called it his concession to instant fame. Maddox told us he'd bought it on the installment plan and so far all he really owned was one sleeve and the inside of the pocket—not the cloth of the pocket, but the hole, the air.

Kolodny had only his scarf to retrieve. He always had a scarf, circling his neck with both ends hanging down. It made him look French or Russian. He said he wore it so he could imagine it was a full head of hair hanging down to his belt.

They left together.

"C'mon," Mark said to me. His guitar case swung gently at the end of his arm.

"She's staying with me," said Strobe.

Mark often walked with me. Usually we were quiet, but sometimes he made me laugh with his offbeat remarks. But I never told him where I lived. I never invited him in. And I never accepted his invitation to go home with him.

"I'll wait for her," he said. The guitar made wider arcs. That meant Mark was anxious.

"No," said Strobe.

They looked at one another. It was a strange moment for me. I felt I was far away, watching myself watching two men watching one another watching me. What did they want? What did I want?

"Don't do this to me," Mark said. I didn't know who he was talking to. It didn't matter. He disappeared.

"He's in love with you," Strobe said. "Milk or lemon?"

"Neither."

"I thought you took—"

"Neither you nor him," I said. "I don't want you and I don't want him."

86

"Who asked?" Strobe drank his tea and looked at me through the fog of steam.

Why had I said it? It's true. No one had asked. I was either turning paranoid or proud, depending on how you looked at it.

"So what do you want?" I asked him—smart-assedly, as Jeffrey would say, to cover my smart ass.

"I want you to move in here."

"You gotta be kidding!" I reached for my virtue without thinking. What a nerve! Who did he think I was?

Strobe leaned over the table and grabbed my wrist. He put his face closer to mine than it had ever been. His eyes weren't just two different colors but many, each distinct but each like shattered glass.

"I don't want to be your lover," he said. "I don't want to be anybody's lover. I've told you before—my flesh is mine, I don't share. What I need you here for is to get our music together. We have to have songs. Now! Immediately! This is our chance. Do you know how fast we can break through? We have a record company ready to sign us. Mitch is ready to get us gigs and then organize the tour when the record is out. He's going to spring us to a video and get it over to RTV and see if they'll put it into rotation. He's got six acts with them now. And he says we can be the biggest. But we gotta have a single. We gotta have twelve singles. We need your songs, Judy. And I need you to stay here to write them."

"I live by myself," I said.

"You've told me that before," he said. "Don't you have parents?"

He'd asked me about them before too. I'd never said a word about them. But now I told him. He ought to know, if we were going to be roommates.

"I used to have parents. They died three years ago. They live in the same apartment I do, but when Jeffrey died, they did too. They were like balloons and the air that filled them was the life of my brother. So when he died, they were empty. They aren't real. I don't see them when I see them. And they don't see me. It's like I don't exist. I go my own way. That's how we all want it. They can't lose me if I'm already gone."

"Then come here," he said.

"I'm getting out of here." I hadn't touched my tea. So there I was, all in a huff, offended and enticed and confused and hurt to think that he wanted me there just so he could suck songs out of me. And I stopped to take a sip of tea so he wouldn't have gone to the trouble of making it for nothing!

Maybe I wanted him to stop me from leaving. But he didn't. He just watched me as I made sure my pants were tucked into my boots all the way around.

31

When I hit Lispenard Street and headed toward the subway, I felt myself being held back, held back, a wind against me, except there was no wind.

It was a very strange sensation. I was in the hands of the night. And I was scared.

Just as I was about to break into a run to try to get out of the grip of this thing that was making my legs heavy and my head light, I heard soft music behind me. A *plink plink plink* of unamplified strings, almost dead except for the life in the fingers that moved them so delicately.

I knew the sound. I was drawn to it. What was this, the Pied Piper of SoHo? I felt like following the sound. I really did.

And then a sweet, high, cracked voice began to sing:

I have seen you, walking through the night,
invisible, to the naked eye.
I have known you, in the dark that knows no
    light,
you let our love die, you let our love die.

It was "Alone (Alone Again)." It was one of my songs!

"Mark?" I said.

He stepped from the shadows then, his guitar around his neck. He looked a little strange. His eyes were glassy but wide open. He might have been asleep, staring at the moon.

"How do you do that?" I asked.

"What?"

"It's like that time in the park when you made the

money fly across the meadow. This time you made me stop in my tracks. It was like a wind blowing me back."

"Toward me," he said.

"Whatever." It was a cold word. Why do we have to use cold words to tell people not to love us as much as they do?

He didn't seem to notice. "It's the power of the music," he explained.

He plucked the strings. It was another song of mine. But I didn't budge.

"It's not working this time." He smiled. He had such a sweet face. He wore a bandanna around his neck, and his smile grew so large that his neck grew small and the bandanna, loosened, fell into his shirt collar.

Then his face grew grim. "But if I could plug it in, I could kill you with it."

I'd never seen him like that. Something was the matter. "Take it back," I said. That's what I used to say to Jeffrey when he said something mean. Except when Jeffrey did it, it was always to try to get me to be better than I'd been. It was never to hurt me.

I went to him. "What's the matter with you? What is it with you? You wait for me down here. You do this voodoo on me with your guitar. You laugh one minute and you tell me you want to kill me the next. And you have this really weird look on your face, like your eyes are popping out. What's the matter with you, Mark? It can't be just . . ."

I knew it wasn't. It wasn't just that he wanted to be more than my friend and less than my brother. He was high.

"What are you on?"

"Tabweiser." He threw his head back and laughed. And he put his hand into his back pocket and pulled out a little bottle of vodka. "Vant some?" he asked like a Russian.

I shook my head and pushed the bottle down so he wouldn't have any either. "Come on," I said, and took his arm like a lady with her man. "Let's take a walk." I had to help him zip up his guitar in its case first. He was drunker than I thought. "The fly is stuck," he said, when he couldn't maneuver the zipper around the tuning pegs.

"Very funny."

"Vant some?"

This time I hit his hand, and the bottle went flying. He watched it like a kid who sees his teddy bear leaving a car window at sixty miles per hour.

"Vell, vhat do you know?" I said as the bottle smashed.

"Aha," he said, happy again, "I see ve come from ze same country."

Now we walked.

"Remember that Russian kid?" I said.

"In first grade?" he said, as if we had grown up together. Don't I wish.

"Don't I wish," I said. "I'm talking about that kid Andrei Berezhkov."

"Oh, him!"

"Do you know who I'm talking about?"

Mark looked ashamed. At least he could close his eyes now. "No."

"That Russian kid who wrote to President Reagan that he hated Russia and he wanted to stay here and then they got him to go home and the last thing he said was—"

" 'Say hi to Mick Jagger'!" said Mark, hopping up and down next to me in his excitement.

"Yeah. And when they asked him why the last person he wanted to say hello to and good-bye to was Mick Jagger, he said—"

" 'Because I love him'!" This time he nearly pulled off my arm. " 'Because I love him.' Like I love you, Judy. Like I love you."

So? He was drunk.

"We all love our rock stars," I said. "Come on, Mark. I'll walk you to the subway." I let him lean on me.

"Where do you live, Judy? How come you never tell me where you live?"

"I'm between homes," I said. "Between lives."

"What about your parents?"

"I don't have any parents."

"Are they dead?" Tears filled his eyes.

I nodded. "Why are you crying?" I asked.

"I feel so sorry for you."

"Don't bother." I let him wipe away his own tears. "What about your parents?"

"They're wonderful." To judge from the sad look on his face, they couldn't have been that wonderful. "Lucky you."

We went our separate ways.

32

Of course I moved in with Strobe. Me and my drum. Me and Jeffrey.

And not just us. We all did. The whole band.

Things got pretty intense pretty fast.

Mitch Sunday got us signed with Edgar Lieberman at Entity. We didn't get any money to carry around in our pockets. But we got enough to make a record, and he gave us only two months to make it. One month to write more songs for it. And to learn the songs. To perfect the songs. To make them part of Wedding Night. Two months to come up with music good enough so we wouldn't be ashamed to be permanent. On the record.

Mitch got us more money to produce the record than we would have gotten ourselves, because he shopped us around. He told Edgar he was taking us to Columbia and Elektra and to see David Geffen. But he actually only took us to see a woman named Rose Marino, who ran Aristotle Records and used to work for Edgar and had left Entity and had taken some of their biggest acts with her, like Scuz and Black Hole and Frieda and the Underarms (the only girl group I would ever consider playing with) and Milton Friedman, that sexiest of all black singers who made Prince look like someone out of the Pubes.

Edgar hated Rose. And Rose loved Wedding Night. Mitch made a secret tape of her reaction to our audition. And so when Mitch told Edgar that Rose had loved us, and Edgar said, "I don't believe Rose Marino has the taste to appreciate a raw talent like yours," Mitch took his perfect cue and asked Edgar if he could use his tape machine, and Edgar said he didn't need to hear us play, he knew how good we were, and Mitch told him to listen anyway, and he did. He listened to a tape of Rose Marino saying "You're the hottest new band I've heard since U2." "How do I know she's talking about you?" Edgar asked. Mitch had him figured perfectly. He just turned the tape back on: "He sings better than Bono, and he's got even more charisma." "How do I know she's talking about Strobe here?" said the skeptical Edgar. So Mitch hit him with the clincher. Rose's unmistakable Westchester voice came out of the giant Azore speakers in Edgar's office saying, "But maybe the greatest thing you got going for you is this girl drummer."

Edgar signed us on the spot.

Mitch started to work with Edgar's people to arrange a tour for us to promote our first record. We weren't big enough to tour on our own. So they had to find us a smash Entity artist or group who would be touring at the same time and we could open for.

They found Nick Praetorious, Entity's biggest star by far, just about the hottest act in America, and supposedly the prettiest, baddest boy in all of rock and roll, who went through girls like time through a clock, as Jeffrey used to say.

And Mitch talked to the head of programming at RTV. When he met us, and heard us play at Strobe's, he said that if we could capture our intensity on video, he would put us right into the rotation.

"But I'd want to see more of *her*," he said.

I ducked.

So we all lived together and created our music together.

I was right in the middle of everything, because Strobe insisted I had to write more songs for the album. He sometimes watched me while I composed. It was the only thing I'd ever amazed him with. Because the way most people wrote at the piano or the guitar, I wrote at the drums. I'd have a piece of music paper taped to one of my toms, and I'd use my fingers and my feet to tap out a rhythm behind the words as they came to me, and the melody behind that. I always wanted the rhythm before the tune. Drummers are like that.

Strobe would kneel about fifteen feet away, staring at me as I went into one of my fits of composition, talking the words to myself and sticking beats into them, usually not the sort of beats you would expect for the kinds of words they were, and gradually singing the words as I went over and over them and either matched or mismatched the melody to the rhythm and the meaning of the words. I liked love songs and sad songs to be rockers sometimes, like "Alone (Alone Again)" and "You Always Love the One You Hurt," and I liked certain possible up-tempo songs, like "Brother," to come off really slow and sloppy and kind of always pulling at the reins of expectation. Against the grain. Rock is art, and if Jeffrey taught me one thing, it's that in art and in life you have to go against the grain. Otherwise you end up indistinguishable from the wall behind you.

By the time I'd be getting toward finishing the rough of a new song, the other guys would usually end up around Strobe, listening to me fuss with it and looking at me as if they thought I was some kind of alien. I loved it. They couldn't put me together with my songs. Nobody could. I was the kid girl drummer who wrote some sassy, grown-up, take-a-walk songs of disillusionment and despair (as Vic Garbarini wrote in *Musician* in his intro to the famous interview he did with me). You wouldn't know it to look at me, thank goodness. It was like meeting a famous writer who looks like he couldn't get a job collecting money in the exact-change lane, and you know that inside that head are stories that'll make your skin catch fire.

Against the grain.

So they'd listen and maybe make a few suggestions

and say what they thought, which was usually that it would be a hit, and then Irwin would grab the pieces of paper I wrote the song on and take them over to the piano and write out his part and Maddox's part and Mark's part, though he knew enough by now to leave Mark some real room to maneuver, and a line for Strobe to sing.

The problem was that Strobe *couldn't* sing some of the songs. Or he could, but he refused to.

"You're writing these for a woman. A man can't sing these songs. How can I sing 'Two Kinds of Men'?" He went into a high voice:

There are two kinds of men in this world for me,
there are men you love and there are men you
    flee,
so what I want to know is why the ones who love
    you
are the ones with whom you want nothing to do.

Nothing to do,
nothing to do,
get out of my life
because you make me blue,
and they say, "Baby,
how I long for you,"
and they say, "Baby,
for my whole life through,
I'll never love anybody else but you,
because you melt my heart,
because you fill my eyes,

because you stop me from tellin'
all my jealous lies,
you bring me peace
to the middle of my life,
I would die to be your husband,
would you kill to be my wife?"

There are two kinds of men in this world for me,
there are men who keep you trapped and there
*   are men who set you free,*
so what I want to know is why the ones who shut
*   you down*
are the ones who can afford to take you out on
*   the town,*
and what I want to know is why the ones who
*   use the knife*
are the ones you want to live with for the rest of
*   your life.*

Nothing to do,
nothing to do,
get out of my life
because you make me blue,
and they say, "Baby,
I'm about to lose my mind,"
and they say, "Baby,
how'm I ever gonna find
a woman like you to fill my heart,
a woman like you to melt my eyes,
I know that we can never be apart
because I hear you tellin' me

all your jealous lies.
You bring despair
to the middle of my life,
I would kill to be your husband,
will you die to be my wife?"

While Strobe sang, Mark improvised a blues line behind him. It was just what I wanted. Mark and I were born from the same musical gene.

Strobe finished and looked around.

"Heavy song," said Maddox.

"It's sick, if you ask me," said Irwin. "I love it." He gave me a hug. He was round and smelled like a grapefruit, which was very refreshing in the sweaty world of rock.

"But it isn't for me to sing," said Strobe. "And neither is 'Brother' or 'Woman of the Spheres' or 'Your Place or Mine?'"

"You can change 'Your Place or Mine?' into a guy's song," I said. "'Your place or mine, *girl*,/Your place or mine?/I feel real fine, *girl*,/I feel real fine. . . .'" I sang, changing "boy" to "girl."

"Not the point," said Strobe. "That's a woman's song. So are most of the others. You're writing about yourself, Judy. 'Woman of the Spheres.' That's a song about a girl drummer. I'm not a girl drummer. I'm a male singer. I can't sing your songs."

"I'll write some other songs," I said.

"That's not the point," Strobe said.

Oh, no. I knew what he was getting at. "I'm not

trying to move in on you," I said, hoping that I could make him think I was, so he'd forget the whole thing about my songs and who was going to sing them.

But he didn't.

"You've got to sing some of these yourself," he said.

"I don't know how to sing."

"There's only one way to find out."

"Who do you think I am, Phil Collins?"

He drew me into the midst of them. My band. My boys. My family. "I think you're going to be the star of this band."

I wanted to run away. But they encircled me. "I won't get up and sing!" I could feel fear and tears rising in me.

"We'll mike you. Just sit back there. These songs are too good to throw out because I can't sing them. I didn't write them. You did. You wrote them, so you've got to sing them. Now let's get going."

Everyone moved into place. But where was Strobe's place now?

"What about you?" I asked him as I walked past him on my way to my kitchen to play my pots and pans.

"We can sing duets." I looked into his eyes. They were calm, unshattered. He seemed to trust me.

" 'Woman of the Spheres,' " he said. "Let's see if this girl can sing."

I wanted to ruin my little audition. But the way those guys played my song, I had to sing it. I had never heard my amplified voice. It was like another person. And she gave me quite a thrill.

I sang my heart out.

Hey, mister, won't you let me in the door,
I got something for you.
Hey, mister, won't you let me in the door,
By the time I'm through with you
I'm gonna have you on the floor.

Hey, mister, I got something that you want
Something that you need,
Something that you long for.
Hey, mister, won't you take a little peek.
Open up the door and you'll see that I'm not
    wrong for
You. You. No, I'm not wrong for you.

Oh, you can't see it.
And you can't feel it.
And you can't touch it.
And you can't even get near it.
But you sure can hear it.
It's hot! It's hot! It's hot hot hot!

Hey, brother, don't be frightened of my size,
It's not your heart I'm after
Or your muscular thighs.
I just want you to hear me,
To open up your ears,
There's not a woman alive who's not more than
    she appears.

101

But there's only one woman who's the woman of
the spheres.

Oh, you can't see it.
And you can't feel it.
And you can't touch it.
And you can't get near it.
But you sure can hear it.
It's hot! It's hot! She sure can play it hot!

"Great song," said Irwin.

"It sure *is* hot," said Maddox.

Mark just stood there, shaking his head at me and blinking his eyes, as if he couldn't believe me and he'd never seen me before.

Strobe said, "Forget it."

I thought it would be what I wanted to hear. Forget it, Judy. You can't sing. Go back behind your drums behind the band. Keep hiding, little girl. You don't have to come out into the world. You don't have to show people who you are.

But it wasn't. I wanted him to like my song. I wanted him to like my singing. I wanted him to think I could do it.

"What's the matter?" I asked.

"It's weak. You're weak. You have a *nice* voice. But a nice voice isn't enough. Do you know how many nice voices there are in the world? But you're too shy. You're holding back. Your heart isn't in it."

"My heart is in *here*." I hit my chest with my drumstick.

102

"Well, when you sing, your heart has to go out *there*." Strobe swung his long arms into the world.

"I don't know how to do that. How do you do it?" I screamed.

"I thought you'd never ask."

33

Strobe taught me how to sing. He taught me how to do vocal exercises, running scales while holding my tongue between my thumb and my first finger. He taught me how to modulate my voice, to find its sweetness and its coarseness. He taught me how to work with the rhythm of a song and not always to sing on beat. He played records for me. Not rock records. But Frank Sinatra records. Ella Fitzgerald records. Sarah Vaughan records. He played me an old bluesman named Robert Johnson and then Billie Holiday and showed me how the two of them shared the same tradition. I heard the same song sung by different singers, and how they stressed different words, made different sounds of the same words, and used the bands behind them.

He also taught me how to use my body, not just to produce sound but to accompany it, whether I was sitting behind the drums or standing all alone onstage. And while he taught me this, he held me, his hands on my hands, his arms around my arms, while we both sang my songs and we seemed like one body pouring forth all the suffering and desire that he told me I wrote about and that made my songs so real.

He showed me how to duet with Mark, me holding the cordless mike and singing, Mark strapped into Shakespeare and the two of us doing the eternal dance of singer and guitarist, heads together, bodies apart, bodies together, rushing at each other from opposite ends of the stage, meeting and embracing without touching, and singing our music, me with my voice and Mark with his guitar.

Strobe was merciless. He made me do things over and over. He stripped me naked of all my inhibitions. Yet he warned me: "Bare your soul. But never give it up."

"How can I do that?" I couldn't believe I could really show people who I was and still be me.

"You can do it," he said. "You can give everything you have."

"And still have anything left?" That's what I was afraid of. That I would have nothing left. Like Jeffrey. Nothing left and nowhere to go and nothing else to be. Just like Jeffrey.

"Not just anything," he answered. "You can give everything you have, and when you're done, you can have more than you began with."

I shook my head. It didn't seem possible.

"It's true," he said. "You can come out of hiding, Judy."

"When?"

Now it was Strobe who shook his head. It wasn't up to him, he was saying. He had taught me all he could teach. It was up to me.

34

We made a demo tape of our songs and brought it to Edgar Lieberman at Entity Records.

He had a huge office with gold records all over the walls, and in the spaces between the gold records there were pictures of him with all his stars.

It was strange to see photos of this older man surrounded by boys in makeup and wet suits and shirts opened to their knees and girls in butch haircuts with their arms around him, pretending for the camera to be whispering something into his ear. Something Mr. Lieberman didn't seem to be hearing.

But the picture of him with Nick Praetorious was different. Mr. Lieberman looked more like he wanted to be Nick's father than the man who ran his record company. He seemed to want Nick to like him. He had his arm around Nick's shoulders and was looking into Nick's beautiful face. But Nick was looking somewhere else, not at the camera exactly, but at the photographer. Except the way the picture was taken, *you* were the photographer. And he was looking at you.

I wondered if Nick Praetorious would ever look at me that way. I wondered if I would ever want him to. It's not that he wasn't my type. I didn't have a type. I didn't want to have a type. I still wasn't ready for a man, especially someone like him, with a terrible reputation for treating women like he was a spider and his arms were the web. So why was I even thinking about him? Why did I feel that, just hanging on the wall inside a picture frame, all brazen in his silence and cocky in his confidence, he exerted some power over me? Was he doing this to me, or was I doing this to myself?

Mr. Lieberman saw me staring at Nick's picture and misunderstood my interest and said kindly, "I don't expect it's going to be too long before you're up there, Judy."

"I don't like to have my picture taken." That wasn't quite true. I *hated* to have my picture taken. I never knew what to do with my mouth. My eyes would burn. I would feel like putting my hands up in front of my face.

Mr. Lieberman laughed. "You'll get used to it." Then he listened to our demo on the incredible equipment he had in his office. He played it at a volume so high I thought my own drums were inside my head. And when my voice filled the room, I jumped and looked around to see if pieces of myself were stuck to the walls.

No one said anything while the tape was on. And no one said anything when it was over. I didn't know whether Mr. Lieberman had liked it. He just sat there shaking his head.

Finally Strobe couldn't take it anymore. "Is your head moving like that in wonderment or dismissal?" he asked.

"The perfect way to ask a difficult question," said Irwin, who never seemed to get bothered by anything. I guess once you walked out on Carnegie Hall and a solo career, everything else fell into perspective.

Maddox was the opposite. He could never relax. He sat there fidgeting with the cushion on his chair and said to Mr. Lieberman in the street-black voice he sometimes used to scare people, "Don't be shaking yo' head at me, man."

Mark just sat there saying nothing. He had a smile on his face and was looking at me, which was what he usually did.

As for me, I figured it was over for us. Mr. Lieberman got to hear dozens of tapes a day. There were tapes piled up on his desk. And the phones were always ringing, making their strange cricket sound. And I knew that on the other end of every one of those calls was a musician or a manager calling to beg Mr. Lieberman to sign up his act, or just to listen to his demo, just to be in the position we were in now, to be lucky enough to get so far as rejection.

I got up to leave.

"Where are you going, Judy?" Mr. Lieberman rose and headed with me toward the door. I thought he was going to show me out, but instead he stood with his back against the door, blocking my way. "I don't mean to keep you in suspense," he said. "And, yes, I was shaking my head in wonderment. That's a fine way to put it. Wonderment. You are a wonderful band. But even more than that, you have wonderful material. Your songs are really special. Most unusual. 'Your Place or Mine?' Very shocking. Very. What an ending! And 'Alone (Alone Again)'—a great, sad love song, especially the way you play it—fast and loud instead of slow and mournful. We always need great, sad love songs. For all the bitterness in the world. And 'The Band Never Dances'—every album should have a song about playing rock and roll, the boys really love songs about bands and music and girls. And 'Let's Get It Together (Before We Break Apart)'—another nice love song. And 'Feel So Bad ('Bout Not Feelin' Bad)' is a terrific antilove song. Every album should have an antilove song. That's how I feel about it. And 'You Always Love the One You Hurt'—very deep, very deep. 'Woman of the Spheres'—another great music song. They're going to love that one, Judy. Hot, hot, hot. And 'The Girl Inside the Girl'—what girl in the world isn't going to feel that song was written especially for her? And 'Brother.' What are we going to do about 'Brother'? That's maybe the most brilliant song you've got here, fellas. But I don't know. It's so controversial. It's so sad. How can anything be so sad? How can anything be as sad as this?" And with that, Mr. Lieberman began to sing some of my song "Brother."

Come back, come back, come back to life,
I miss your crazy ways,
Come back, come back, come back to life,
And I'll be sure it stays

[and here's where the big bang came in and I power-drummed the next two lines]

The kind of life you want it to be,
The kind of life you want to live with me.
The kind of life you want it to be,
The kind of life you want to live with me.
The kind of life you want it to be,
The kind of life you want to live with me.

I was amazed. One listen, and Mr. Lieberman could sing my song. He had a terrible voice, but he wasn't afraid to belt it out. Here he was, this famous businessman who controlled half the music world, and he was leaning up against the door to his office, to be sure we wouldn't leave, singing a song I'd written.

"How could you remember it?" I asked. "You heard it only once."

"That's the secret of all great pop tunes. You hear them once, and you think you're never going to get them out of your mind. Then you hear them twice, and you never *do* get them out of your mind. They keep

109

you awake at night. They drive you nuts. But like most things that drive you nuts, you love them."

"So are we ready?" said Strobe.

"You're ready." Mr. Lieberman went over to Strobe. "I even like some of *your* songs." He smiled. So did Strobe, though I could tell he didn't want to. "You've got more than enough for an album. I'm going to send you down to Montserrat to record. Maybe put some color in your cheeks." He laughed. We all laughed, except for Strobe, who probably couldn't imagine having to subject his perfectly white skin to the sun. "And I want you to get this down fast. I want you to go on the road behind this album. I want you to open for Nick Praetorious."

35

We went to Montserrat, which is an island in the West Indies. There's a famous recording studio there that is run by a man named George Martin, who used to produce the Beatles. George Martin wasn't there when we were, but we kept feeling that his spirit was, and that made us try very hard. We could also feel the spirit of the legendary Police, who had recorded there, and we liked to think of playing our music in the same room where Sting and Andy Summers and Stewart Copeland had played theirs. I really liked the way Stewart played the drums, and it helped me to think of him and some of his African rhythms and particularly his Caribbean rhythms, which I incorporated from my memory of Stewart's playing but even more from that beautiful little island, which is shaped like a pear and has a row of volcanic mountains running down the middle, covered with jungle. On every side there is the sea, with sheer cliffs going down to black sands leading into blue water. The sand was as black as Nick Praetorious's hair, and the sea as blue as his eyes. I knew that from pictures of him, before we'd even met.

The band worked like crazy for nearly a month. Strobe had convinced Mr. Lieberman that he, Strobe, should produce us, so he did, and he was in complete control, which was just as well, since Strobe was the only one of us who really knew how to work the sound engineers and all the other technicians and to make them see the vision he had of Wedding Night.

We went over and over our songs, adding to them, mostly taking away from them, playing them first one way, then another, then another, playing with tempo, with rhythm, with the color of the sounds, with the voicings of our instruments, with the words and the music and the very presence of ourselves within the songs.

"You inhabit the song, when you're a musician, the way the song is supposed to inhabit the person who listens to it," Strobe said. "And if *you* don't get far enough into it to inhabit it, then there's no way that

111

song is going to get inside the people you're playing for. So you might as well pack it right up and go home."

We fought each other. We really did. We screamed and we swore and we each went through silent periods when we wouldn't speak to anyone else and we told one another that this was the worst experience of our lives.

But we also had the greatest time in our lives. We refined our music. We worked and worked and worked on four bars of music, eight bars, *one* bar, over and over and over again, and then we fit those bars or that one bar into what we already had, and we played *that* over and over and over. And then we laid it down on tape, and we listened to it, and we nodded, and we shook our heads, and we went back and we changed it a little here and a little there, and we listened to it again and . . . and we heard it as if it had been played by someone else! We heard it as we stood there behind the console tired and hot and played out and sung out and just generally lived out, and it was right. So we hugged and we kissed and we jumped up and down.

Until Strobe said, "Let's try it again, boys and girls."

When it got to be too much in the studio, we sat in the villa that Entity Records owned, where we lived while we were there. Or we took walks in Plymouth, which is the largest town on Montserrat, where we watched men weave Sea Island cotton and wandered on Parliament Street, where we bought things like mango chutney and pawpaw jam, and then went to the Grasshopper Bar, where I would order a Tab and the others would drink Perk's Punch, which was a famous local drink. I tried it once and thought it tasted like medicine. Mark swore he loved it.

It was like being with my brothers. Not my brother brother, because there was only one Jeffrey. But still, here I was, the one girl in a band of guys, one young girl, and they took great care of me and made me feel I wasn't even as much of a stranger as I sometimes felt. Out of place. Not just in the band. Out of place in life. Especially since Jeffrey died. Off to the side. Alone. Or out in back, watching everybody else, listening to everybody else, but never saying anything, though always my heart would beat to the rhythm of the life I watched and heard, and my drums would beat to the rhythm of the music.

On the day we finished laying down all the songs we were going to need and more, Mark asked me to take a walk with him.

We went out along a place called Galway's Soufrière, which was really this kind of slice in the ground that went up alongside a volcano. It smelled like rotten eggs at first, but then we got used to it. We actually went right into that slice, as if we were going to walk into the middle of the earth, or into hell, and we could see golden seams in the sliver of earth, with gas hissing out of them.

There were little holes right in the surface of the ground. Mark took my hand and led it toward one of those holes. It was like a contest, to see which one of us would flinch first from the heat. It got hotter and hotter the closer he pushed our hands toward the hole. But that just made us hold our hands together more tightly. We could feel the whole planet purse its lips into this tiny hole and blow at us, as if it wanted to melt our hands together for all eternity.

Then, all of a sudden, the hissing stopped, the wind from the throat of the earth stopped blowing, and we couldn't feel a thing, except our hands together, suspended in the cool mountain air over a world that had stopped breathing.

The volcano slept. Beneath our feet was bare rock or melted clay. Nothing grew. There was nothing alive here except for us.

Mark continued to hold my hand.

I continued to hold his.

He looked so different without his guitar. He almost always had Shakespeare with him. Not just in the studio but when we went around town too. He was still like the boy we'd found in Central Park, when he played his music for the birds and the air, waiting for his band to come along.

Now he had a band, just like me, but he still carried his guitar, as if he couldn't quite believe it.

Me too. I still carried around my desire to be me and me alone. To be left alone. To be invisible. To know everything but to be unknown. Being in the band hadn't changed that. Singing in the band hadn't changed that. I felt *better* than I ever had before, or at least since Jeffrey was alive and we lived our lives together in the same house, almost in the same room, and he showed me what it was like to be a person who hid from nothing, even if he hid everything, just like me, behind all his costumes and in his search for the real Jeffrey, the Jeffrey who would be comfortable just being Jeffrey. The Jeffrey he never found.

I felt better, but I was still afraid of losing myself. I still kept a tight grip on myself.

So when Mark put his arms around me up there on the top of the world, with the gas beginning to rise up again around us, I could let him do it, yes, I could. But I could not put my arms around him. I could feel him yearning for me to do that. But I could not put my arms around him.

He let me go finally. He tried to make light of it. He pretended he had Shakespeare in his hands and he strummed it, he picked it, he started to slam his right hand against the imaginary strings.

His lips moved, but he didn't say a word. I couldn't tell if he was actually mouthing a song or some kind of message to me, which he couldn't bring himself to say, or if he was just screaming silently.

He held that imaginary guitar against his body and between me and him. He slammed it and banged it and started to jump up and down just the way he did onstage, and his huge stage smile spread across his face.

Up there on Galway's Soufrière, Mark The Music played for the whole world. He didn't have a guitar. He didn't have a band. He didn't have me.

No one heard him. Except me. And all I could hear was the sadness in his heart.

I knew that Mark had taken me up there in order to hold me in his arms. He didn't want to tell me how he felt. He wanted to show me. He wanted to get away from the rest of the band. Away from Strobe.

Mark thought I was in love with Strobe. But I wasn't. Not the way Mark thought. Strobe was my brother. Strobe was my father. Strobe was all men to me except for the man who would see into my body and make me forget myself, who would hide me in his arms and at the same time bring me out of hiding.

Besides, Strobe didn't want to be loved. He wasn't like me. I wanted to be loved. But I still didn't let anybody love me. Jeffrey was the last person I let love me. And that hadn't been enough—not for either of us.

But Mark loved me anyway. I didn't know why. Why would anyone love me? Sometimes I thought I knew. I was a very hip girl drummer in the best new rock band in the world, and we were about to have our first record and go on our first tour and there I was, hidden in the back of the band, beating its blood through its veins with my drums. I was a mystery. People always loved mysteries.

But they didn't love Judy. How could they? They

didn't know me. No one would ever know me. I wouldn't let them.

Mark wouldn't take my hand on the way down. I needed him to. I was sliding on the rock and slipping in the clay. I needed someone to hold on to. But Mark had turned a corner. Mark had stopped being a boy. He had put his arms around me and had probably never felt so alone in his life.

We came down from the mountain like two strangers, while all around us dirty water boiled its throaty music.

36

We left Montserrat and returned to New York. We had a good sixteen songs laid down. We loved them all, but we knew that only ten would be on the album.

"Don't worry," Mitch Sunday told us. "We'll just put the extras in the vault. It's like having money in the bank. Everybody records songs they don't release. Or they don't release right away."

Strobe agreed with him. And Irwin and Maddox didn't care one way or the other—they were just along for the ride, they said, they were having the times of their lives and didn't worry about anything except playing well.

It was harder for me and Mark to accept the fact

that some of the songs wouldn't go on the album. It was as if they would disappear.

And when Mr. Lieberman told Strobe that "Brother" wasn't going to be included, and Strobe told me, I wanted to cry. "But he *loved* that song. He said it was one of the great pop tunes. Remember how he even sang some of it, Strobe? Remember?"

We were in our place on Lispenard Street. Strobe had made me some tea. He must have thought it would help when he broke the bad news. The others were out somewhere. We were taking a break from our rehearsals for the tour.

Strobe sat down with me and picked up my teacup and blew across the surface of the tea. He had become fatherly like that. I loved that about him.

"He still likes the song. But he also said it was controversial. That's one thing, Judy. And he said it was sad. That's another. He thinks it's *too* sad. But the worst problem is, it's too long."

"Too long?"

"It's too long for radio play; it's too long for a video. And he says that if we just stick it in the middle of an album, it's going to disappear anyway and it's going to take up too much of one side, and we'll have to eliminate two other songs."

"I really love that song. That's one of my best songs."

"We can play it on tour, Judy. We can do a full version of it onstage."

He thought I'd love to hear that. But the very

thought of it made me scared. It was such a personal song. It was a song that no one in the band but me could sing. And I couldn't imagine getting up in front of thousands of people and singing "Brother."

I shook my head. Strobe thought I was still disagreeing with the decision not to put the song on the album. But I was just thinking about how I didn't ever want to have to get up from behind my drums.

"But listen to this," he said. "Lieberman wants to call the album *The Band Never Dances*."

"He does?" I was really surprised. We all had thought it was just going to be called *Wedding Night*.

"He loves the song. And he loves the name of the song. 'The Band Never Dances.' "

"That's what Jeffrey used to say."

"Truer words were never spoken." Strobe got up. "Let's get back to work."

I looked around. "But we're the only ones here."

"When has that ever stopped us? And you're still not ready?"

"For what?"

"To be a star."

"I don't want to be a star."

"Everybody wants to be a star."

"I don't want to be a star," I repeated.

"Why not?"

"Because I don't want people to start trying to find out everything about me. There isn't even anything to find out anyway. I'm a girl who plays the drums whose brother killed himself. That's all."

"That's not all." Strobe looked at me intently, as if he were trying to convince me that there was more to me than met my own eye.

"I don't want to be in the spotlight," I said. "I like it in the dark. I like it in the back. I like it where I can look out and see everything and nobody can look in and see me."

"What are you hiding from, Judy?"

"Who said I was hiding?"

Strobe almost laughed before his mouth turned down and he took my arms in his hands. I thought he was going to shake me like a father shakes his little girl when he can't stand her any longer. But he just held on to me and said, "What are you hiding from?"

"Disappointment," I said.

"Ah, yes," said Strobe. He still held my arms in his hands. I realized that was his version of a hug. "Disappointment."

37

Our touring schedule appeared in the On the Road column in *Rolling Stone*. It said WEDDING NIGHT/ NICK PRAETORIOUS and under that a list of cities that looked to me like the names of far-off planets and I thought of myself flying between them with my new family and my drums, with nowhere to live now except on the road: Oakland, CA; San Francisco, CA; Seattle, WA; Spokane, WA; Medford, OR; Reno, NV; Fresno, CA; Bakersfield, CA; Las Vegas, NV; Long Beach, CA; Los Angeles, CA; San Bernardino, CA; Albuquerque, NM; Phoenix, AZ; El Paso, TX; Lubbock, TX; Austin, TX; Corpus Christi, TX; San Antonio, TX; Odessa, TX; Oklahoma City, OK; Amarillo, TX; Beaumont, TX; Dallas, TX; Houston, TX; Lafayette, LA; Baton Rouge, LA; New Orleans, LA; Pensacola, FL; Tallahassee, FL; Tampa, FL; Miami, FL; Orlando, FL; Gainesville, FL; Jacksonville, FL; Savannah, GA; Atlanta, GA; Charlottesville, VA; Richmond, VA; Fairfax, VA; Raleigh, NC; Norfolk, VA; Baltimore, MD; Kalamazoo, MI; Detroit, MI; Cleveland, OH; Milwaukee, WI; St. Paul, MN; Rockford, IL; St. Louis, MO; Omaha, NE; Kansas City, MO; Lansing, MI; Ann Arbor, MI; Binghamton, NY; Rochester, NY; Ottawa, CAN; Toronto, CAN; Glens Falls, NY; Springfield, MA; Worcester, MA; Uniondale, NY; East Rutherford, NJ; and New York, NY.

We would be gone just over three months and would have almost no days off. We didn't want days off. All we wanted to do was take off and play our music.

So we waited around for our record to get pressed and distributed. Then, one day, we got on a plane with all our equipment and our manager, Mitch Sunday, and his assistant, and the roadies he'd hired to help us set up and take down and travel, and a publicist from his office, and that was it, nobody else, no girlfriends, no boyfriend, no groupies, nobody else to keep us company, and the plane took off, and we were on our way to rock and roll glory.

I wanted to sit next to Mark on the plane, but ever since Montserrat he had been avoiding me. The more he avoided me, the more I didn't want to avoid him. But that's how things went in life, I knew, so I avoided him too, in case that might make him not want to avoid me so much. Unfortunately, all it led to was that I didn't end up sitting next to him on the plane.

I had Irwin on one side of me and Maddox on the other. That was fine with me. But all they talked about was women: Irwin kept saying how he hoped he would meet his future wife on this trip, and Maddox kept saying how he hoped he would meet every woman in the world *except* for his future wife on this trip.

"I really want to settle down," Irwin said.

"I really want to unsettle down," said Maddox.

They laughed at each other. They slapped hands across me. Then they shook hands in front of me. I stared at their hands clasped right before my eyes. Then I looked at both of them and saw they were inviting me to join their handshake. So I added my hand to the pile, and we all laughed.

"What do you hope to find on this trip, Judy?" Irwin asked.

"Oh, nothing," I said. "Fame. Fortune. The love of my life. Instant immortality. Stuff like that."

"Is that *it*?" asked Maddox.

"No. One more thing."

"What's that?"

"The girl inside the girl," I answered.

"All *right*!" Maddox slapped Irwin's shoulder and the two of them began to sing,

> *'Cause she's the girl,*
> *she's the girl inside the girl,*
> *she's the girl you never find,*
> *not in your heart or in your mind.*

38

The first time I met Nick Praetorious was during our rehearsals for our first show at the Henry J. Kaiser Auditorium in Oakland, California.

We were going to open there for Nick that night, our first on the tour, and we were running through our songs and getting used to the feel of such a big place. It held over ten thousand people, and we'd never played in anything so large, not together, though Strobe said he'd played there years before, in another incarnation. He told us not to worry about size, just to play for ourselves and we'd fill any arena in the world with our sound.

We weren't sure when we were going to meet Nick

Praetorious. Strobe told us he was probably one of those main acts that didn't want to have anything to do with the band that was opening for him.

Nick had a terrible reputation. He had been on the cover of nearly every magazine in America, and they all said he was vain, arrogant, beautiful, brilliant, mean, cold, aloof, sexy, and dangerous.

He was the biggest rock star in the country right then. His records sold millions. His videos alone had launched a whole new video network, RTV, which stood for Rock Television, which was signing up artists to exclusive deals and was going out on regular TV, not cable, and was already more popular than MTV. Nick made a video for every one of his songs, not just for the biggest hits, and he sold the videos one by one as well as in a package. Some of his videos outsold his records. Everyone wanted to see him. Everyone wanted to know him. Everyone wanted him.

Except me. I didn't want him. I just wanted to see him.

The first chance I got was that very afternoon. We were running through our songs and learning how to use that big stage when Mitch Sunday came into the middle of us and held up his hands and said, "Hey, guys, guess who just came in?"

Maddox kept pumping his bass. "You're interrupting my flow, Mitch."

Irwin suddenly launched into "Here Comes the Bride."

I searched the auditorium from my place in the

124

back. I had my drums built up around me. I knew no one could see me. I felt secure.

Strobe stopped singing. "Who is it?"

"Our headliner," said Mitch.

"It's about time," said Strobe.

Mark didn't say anything.

Nick approached down the long central aisle out of the grayness of the back of the auditorium. He had three people with him. Two of them were enormous men who wore skullcaps and whose pants made swishing noises because their thighs rubbed together. The other was a beautiful girl.

Nick leaped up onto the stage. He was famous for his leaps. The two giants with him had such big thighs that they couldn't possibly have leaped up. They had to leave him and come around up the stairs at the sides. They looked worried when they weren't next to Nick. They looked like he owed them money. But I knew they were his bodyguards.

The beautiful girl didn't leap up onto the stage or come around to the side. She just stood there, looking up at Nick.

He looked down at her.

She looked up at him some more. Then she held up her hands to him.

"Jump," he said, and turned his back on her.

The two huge guys bent and lifted her up. She smiled all the way, but I was sure that inside she was either weeping or cursing.

"So this is Wedding Night," Nick didn't say that to

125

anyone in particular. He also didn't walk right toward us. He went to one side, and then to the other. He was checking us out. I hid behind my drums and watched him. He was wearing a purple shirt and black leather pants and low black boots outside his pants. That was it. He didn't wear a headband or a neckerchief or any kind of jewelry, not even a ring. Nothing to detract from his beauty. His black hair was silky and deep like Chinese black hair, smooth to the touch of my eyes. His blue eyes jumped out from beneath his black eyebrows. I realized that they were his jewels. His mouth was mean. It made you want to bite it.

"I just heard your record," he said.

I could tell we were all waiting to hear what he thought of it. But he didn't say anything else about it.

"Which one of you is Strobe?"

As if he couldn't tell. Who could be Strobe, aside from the tall, thin man with the eyes of two colors and streak of white hair and invisible skin and the look of someone who has been dead and come back to life?

When no one answered him, he said to Irwin, "You, you're Strobe."

There stood Irwin, his bald head shining, his two flaps of hair hanging down, his belly nearly resting on his keyboard, and a spontaneous chuckle making his lips wag.

"And you must be Barry Manilow," Irwin said.

That made Maddox laugh. "Wrong guy," he said. "I'm Strobe."

126

"So who's this freaky guy who looks like a ghost?" said Nick.

"I'm Strobe," said Strobe.

Nick ignored him. "So who's that behind there?" He looked over toward my drums. I bent down behind them so he'd never be able to find me.

"That's our drummer." Strobe said it like a secret, but one he was proud of.

"The girl?"

"The girl," Strobe answered.

"Since when can girls play drums?"

I was tempted to show him since when.

He walked back toward my drum kit. I hunched over and tried not to look at him. But he came right at me and stared into my eyes. He stood right in front of me and stared and stared until I found myself sitting up straighter and straighter and I had my head up and was staring right back at him. My eyes burned, and my skin was on fire, but I locked my eyes into his and didn't let go.

Then he smiled. "Pleased to meet you. I'm Nick Praetorious."

He let his hand slide into mine and then he squeezed it very gently.

"Judy Valentine."

At that moment I began to hear a guitar play. It started very softly, playing a beautiful melody that I knew I recognized but I didn't know from where. It wove in and out around the notes, getting louder and louder, and the tune began to come more and more forward until I realized it was one of my songs, "Let's Get It Together (Before We Break Apart)," and it was Mark playing it, doing this fabulous solo version of it that he dug into and tore out of his guitar like his heart from his body.

I looked at Mark. He was hunched over his guitar. I wanted to say, "Mark, don't hide. It's beautiful."

But Mark just melted into his guitar, until my song shrieked in my own ears and then he brought it back to himself softer and softer until I could hardly hear it and then there was silence.

"Incredible," Irwin whispered.

Maddox applauded with one hand against the solid body of his electric bass.

Strobe walked over to Mark and just stood in front of him, shielding him from the world.

Nick still had my hand. He was holding it so hard. There was no way I could get to Mark.

"He was playing that for you," Nick said into my ear. I could smell him, his hair, his skin. I didn't think I'd ever smelled a man before. That was all I could imagine. This was how a man smelled. "He loves you. But I'm going to have you."

He dropped my hand. When I opened my eyes, he was standing back at the front of the stage. His arm was around the beautiful girl. She was kissing his neck.

"I heard your record," he said to us again. "I hope you play better than that in person."

He snapped his fingers at the two huge men, and

128

they followed him and the girl as he leaped off the stage with her. They would follow him to hell, I thought.

I wondered if I would too.

39

We were very nervous that first night. Or at least I was. The stage was dark, the audience was clapping its hands rhythmically, because of course the roadies and the local stagehands were late setting us up and plugging us in, and the audience began to chant, "Nick, Nick, Nick."

We could hear them from the dressing room. The walls were white, except for one of them that was a mirror. It was impossible to hide from it, unless you turned your back on it. I did and ended up staring at a white wall. The other guys walked back and forth in front of the mirror, looking at themselves and then down at their feet. Except for Mark, who just stood in front of the mirror, looking himself up and down, constantly adjusting his formal white shirt with its dozens of pleats down the front, his black suspenders, and his bright-red cummerbund. He was drinking a beer.

I went over to him and said, "That doesn't look like a Tabweiser."

"It isn't. Want a taste?"

Before I could say no, he tilted his head back and drank down the rest of the bottle.

"What's the matter with you?" I asked. "Are you nervous? I'm nervous."

He looked past me toward the door we'd soon be walking through on our way to the stage and what we knew would be instant rock immortality. "Listen to them. 'Nick, Nick, Nick.'" Mark said the name contemptuously. "'Nick, Nick, Nick.' They don't want to hear us. They don't know us. They don't care about us. I don't even know what we're doing here. We should be in the park, playing for the trees. 'Nick, Nick, Nick.' That guy's a creep. Don't you think so, Judy? Nick, Nick, Nick is a creep. Go ahead and say it. Say it!"

But I couldn't say it. I knew I didn't want him to be one. I could still smell him, his skin, his hair. I could feel his hand in my hand and I didn't think the feeling would go away until I held my drumstick and hit one of my cymbals and the world would go away and music would come rushing in to take its place.

I looked into Mark's eyes. Poor Mark. He was so sad. Just when he ought to have been most happy, just when we were about to launch our careers and become the best band in the world, he was all wrapped up in his sadness. I knew it was partly my fault. He was my friend. But he wanted to become my lover. And I couldn't even put my arms around him. I couldn't put my arms around anyone. The only thing

130

I could hold in my arms was the air around my drums.

"I can't," I confessed. "I'm sorry, Mark. I can't say it."

"I don't like you." He turned from me and looked back into the mirror, where his eyes met his eyes and he could see so clearly how beautiful a boy he was and how unhappy.

There was a loud knock on the dressing-room door. "Let's go, Wedding Night! Let's go."

The door opened and a couple of men with long hair motioned us out with the long flashlights they held in their hands. We walked behind them down one long corridor and then another until we got to the side of the stage and they turned on their flashlights and led us onto the dark stage.

"Nick, Nick, Nick," went the cry from the audience.

"Ladies and gentlemen," boomed out a voice over the PA system as we took our places, "won't you join me in giving a rousing Oakland, California, welcome to a new band from New York City, a band that's as hot as its name, Wedding Night!"

As what seemed like millions of lights came on together, with a kind of clacking stutter that we could hear on every side of us, and we were covered in their blazing glow and their heat wrapped itself around our skin, thousands of people in the audience screamed out their disappointment, "Nick! Nick! Nick!" while thousands more booed us. Before we had played a single note.

We tried. We really tried. But we couldn't win

them. That's a thing you know. If I learned anything that night, it was that you *knew* when you didn't get an audience in your grasp.

It wasn't their fault. It wasn't Nick Praetorious's fault. It was ours.

We were frightened. We were inexperienced. We were intimidated.

Worst of all, we were not a band. We were not a family of musicians. We were just five people up there on a stage playing some notes and singing some words.

We thought we were lucky just to get through a song before beginning another. We rushed things. We played too loud and then we played too soft. We jumped around like maniacs on one song and then stood there like dead people on another one. We tried playing solos and then we tried to play duets and then we just ended up trying to drown out our own music by all playing together because we knew, even as we played it, that we didn't want it to exist.

And without our music, we didn't exist.

It was a relief to finish our set. I had sunk lower and lower behind my built-up drum kit as we went from song to song, and when we'd played our last planned number, I was praying they wouldn't ask us for an encore.

But I was surprised that when we came down on the last chord, and Strobe handed his microphone to a roadie, and the lights went crazy above our heads to signal the grand finale of our set, the audience let up a little cheer.

Some of them booed, it was true, but some of them cheered, they cheered for a minute as we took our bows and started to walk off, and then the cheers turned to "Nick, Nick, Nick," and the cheers got louder and louder, and the cries for Nick got louder and louder, and we left the stage with Nick's name sounding in our ears. Just the way we had come in.

Mitch Sunday and some of our roadies were standing in the wings holding white towels for us, which they draped over our necks as we walked by. The same men with flashlights escorted us down the stairs.

Mitch hurried along next to Strobe, saying, "That was great. That was just great. That was great."

Strobe looked down at him. "The truth," he demanded.

"That was great, man."

Strobe stopped. We all stopped. Strobe fastened his eerie eyes on Mitch Sunday and said to him in a hoarse whisper, "It wasn't great. It was poor. And if you want to go on being our manager, then you're either going to have to learn the difference between great playing and bad playing or you're going to have to learn to tell the truth. Now which is it, Mitch? Are you too stupid to know the difference? Or are you lying?"

Mitch let out a nervous laugh. "I'm lying."

Strobe turned in disgust and walked back toward

the dressing room. We followed him like ducks, in a row.

On the way, we passed Nick and his band and a whole bunch of other people, including the two giants and the blond girl and about ten other girls and roadies and men in business suits and worried-looking women in business suits who were saying "Clear the way" and "Are you sure there's enough lime in your Perrier, Nick?" and "What password do you want on the backstage late passes tonight, Nick?" and "Is there anything else you need, anything at all?" Everybody except the band was wearing a plastic pass pinned to their clothes that said NICK PRAETORIOUS: BAND.

Nick was in the middle of all this. He wasn't wearing leather pants now but loose black pants, like a karate master's, and a clean white shirt slit down the front, and a long yellow sash around his waist. His feet were bare. His toes were long and clean and looked very strong, as if they could actually grip the stage and then help him shoot up into the air to do one of his famous leaps.

When he was right next to us, he held up his hand, and his whole entourage just stopped.

"You're an easy act to follow," he said. "Lieberman told me you'd be a tough act to follow. He told me you were going to be a challenge. I need something to bring out the best in me. And you people are going to bring out the worst in me. I heard you. Did you

134

hear you? Because if you did, you know you stink. So now I've got to go out on that stage and try to get rid of the stink. And that means I'm going to stink until I get rid of the stink. And I like to smell sweet all the time. Judy knows that, don't you, Judy? Judy knows how sweet I smell. So if you people keep stinking up my stage, I'm going to call Lieberman and tell him to get rid of you. And you—"

He was looking right at me when Mitch Sunday said to him, "Now wait a minute, Nick. You can't do that. We've got a deal with Lieberman. You can't call him and—"

Nick ignored him completely and said to me, "You meet me backstage after the show. Here's a pass." He snapped his fingers and one of the women handed him a pass. It was blank, and the woman said, "But Nick, what's the password?"

"The password is *Wedding Night.*" Nick laughed. "How's that, Judy? Our password for tonight is *Wedding Night.* Tonight's our wedding night, Judy. As they say on television, be there."

The woman took out a large black felt-tipped pen and wrote WEDDING NIGHT on my pass and handed it to me. Her eyes were as blank as the pass had been. I could tell she had written out hundreds of passes for Nick in hundreds of cities. For hundreds of wedding nights. She didn't know who I was. She didn't care. I was just supposed to do what Nick said, exactly the way she did.

"Share your wedding night with me, not with them," he said. He touched my hand, and then he walked away.

He walked away with all of his people following him, into the continuing cries of "Nick, Nick, Nick," which I hoped were all coming from the audience, though I was afraid some of them were coming from me, inside.

40

When we all got back to the dressing room, I noticed no one looked in the mirror.

Mark sat down with his back pressed against the mirror and his legs arched like a bridge with his guitar, Shakespeare, beneath it. He put his arms on his knees and his head on his arms. His eyes were gone from the world. I could only imagine the pain in his mind, from the music gone wrong tonight and for me gone wrong, running after Nick Praetorious (though I hadn't taken a step that anyone could see).

Irwin and Maddox stood talking near the door. They seemed to want to get out of there. I didn't think they were as upset as the rest of us. Maybe it was because they thought the good music would always come back someday. Maddox had played hundreds of times in clubs where people didn't come to hear him anyway but to see men dressed as women singing about impossible love. And Irwin had played recitals in so many tiny, empty halls that tonight, surrounded by over ten thousand people, he might have felt he at least had had the chance to be appreciated by more people than he ever dreamed possible.

Irwin put his hand on Maddox's shoulder and said, "So where are all the groupies?" He looked around the dressing room. No groupies. Only the group. He shook his head.

"My sentiments exactly," said Maddox.

"How am I going to find a wife if there aren't even any girls?" Irwin now put his head on Maddox's shoulder, pretending to cry.

"Not my sentiments at all." Maddox laughed at Irwin's great desire to meet the girl of his dreams. Irwin laughed too.

"Well, off to the hotel," said Irwin.

Maddox nodded. "It's always lonely on your wedding night."

They started to leave.

"Take Mark with you," Strobe told them.

But what about me? What about Strobe? Was he willing to leave me behind to meet Nick backstage? Or was he planning to be my chaperone?

"No," said Mark into his knees.

"Oh, come on, Mark," said Irwin. He went over to him and held out his hand.

Mark got up in one swift movement and brushed Irwin aside with one arm while he gripped Shakespeare to him with the other. He almost ran for the door.

"Mark, where are you going, Mark?" I called after him. I could see him disappearing. From me. From us.

"Where are *you* going?" he asked me. But he was gone before I could answer with an answer I didn't know or couldn't say.

Strobe looked at the empty, open doorway as if his own child had left home. I thought of Jeffrey. And then of myself, leaving home all my life, or at least since Jeffrey had left, had died. As if my parents didn't exist.

My poor parents. They didn't even know where I was now, that I was on the road. They only knew I didn't live at home. I was a total mystery to them. We were not a family at all.

The look in Strobe's eyes had been the look of a parent. Mark was like his kid.

And when he turned to me, I realized I was too.

"You two go back to the hotel," he said to Irwin and Maddox. "I'm staying here with Judy."

They nodded.

"Home to our lonely beds," said Irwin.

"I wonder what kind of girls they have on TV here," said Maddox. "Hey, maybe they're California girls."

"California girls!" Irwin squealed with delight.

And he and Maddox broke into "California Girls" like two of the most unlikely Beach Boys you'd ever dream of meeting.

138

They went out singing, with their arms around each other's shoulders.

Strobe and I were alone. We both turned around at the same time. I looked at him in the mirror, and he looked at me.

"What are we going to do?"

"We're going to find out what kind of act it's hard to follow."

"Nick?" I was filled with dreadful excitement.

"Let's see how good he is."

41

He was wonderful. From the moment he launched into "Wishbone," his trademark opening, he owned the stage, and he gave it away with each song he sang. People couldn't stay in their seats. Even when he sang a ballad, they stood, on the floor or on their seat cushions or on the armrests, reaching for heaven, reaching for him, their arms entangled in the air, their fingers desperate, their eyes forever on him, Nick.

He wasn't like Wedding Night. He had a different kind of act. It wasn't as straight-ahead rock. His band was bigger. He had horns; a sax player who urged him on, just the way Clarence Clemons does with Bruce; a girl violin player, who made me think of

when Bob Dylan had one, or John Cougar Mellen-
camp, except this girl leaned against Nick when she
played, and her hair fell all over him, and her bow
sawed all around his body. I knew I was like all the
other girls in Kaiser Auditorium, afraid for his life,
hungry for his life, and making a New Year's resolution, never mind how far it was from New Year's, to
learn the violin and lean against Nick Praetorious and
make music together while our clothes burned off
from the contact alone.

He was a great dancer. He was a great singer. But
most of all, he was a great lover. He loved everything
and everybody. He loved his microphone. He loved the
floor. He loved the sash around his waist. He loved his
three black backup singers, who he sometimes stood
behind with his arms around them all. He loved his
band and kept looking coyly and smiling at them. He
loved his songs and sang each one as if it were for the
last time. He loved the lights, which bathed him and
were the envy of all of us. He loved the sweat that fell
from his brow and that he caught on his tongue and
drank like holy water. He loved the noise we made
and the dancing we danced and the girls who fainted
and the boys who imitated him without knowing they
were doing it and the boys who imitated him on pur-
pose, right down to the yellow sash and the way he
penciled his eyebrows. He loved you, and he loved me.
But most of all he loved me.

He couldn't see me. He couldn't know I was there.
But I knew he loved me from the way he sang his

140

songs and the way he sometimes turned toward where I was standing in the roped-off VIP section at the right front of the auditorium, and looked right at me, though I knew he couldn't see me, because I knew you couldn't see a thing from the stage. The lights blinded you and your sweat blinded you and the most you could make out were endless fuzzy heads like some huge blanket laid out for you to fall upon should you grow weak. But I thought, I'm on his mind. He asked me to meet him later. So even while he's up there singing his heart out and the whole world is worshiping him and he knows it, I'm on his mind.

I knew that every girl in that place thought she was on his mind. If only he knew her. If only he could see her (but he could; look, he was looking right at her!). If only he would take the time to get to know her and realize how wonderful she would be for him.

We *all* wanted him. And he wanted all of us. That was his secret. And ours. There was enough love in this huge room to go around to everyone. And it had all come from one place: Nick Praetorious.

When he left the stage after his last encore, and the house lights went up to make the kids stop lighting matches and flicking their Bics at him, the illusion of his love was gone so quickly that girls just sat there in their seats crying and the boys who tried to swagger and dance up the aisles like Nick realized how stupid they looked and just stopped in their tracks and looked around, to be sure no one had seen them trying to be someone they realized they could never be.

Of course a few girls walked down toward the stage instead of toward the back or side exits. I knew who they were and what they wanted.

It was as if Strobe had read my mind. "Groupies are the strangest sign of success. Suddenly people want to make love to you. Since they didn't all want to make love to you before, it can only be the music that's making them want to do it now. The music seduces them, and they think it's somebody's tight pants."

For Strobe, it was always the music. For Strobe, there was only the music. You thought he'd waste away without it. And he thought the world would waste away without it.

"I like his music," I said.

Strobe looked at the stage as if he could still see Nick up there, instead of a crew of stagehands with beer bellies and tractor company hats. "He's good," he said. "We're better."

"So what was the matter with us tonight?"

"Maybe it was because no one could see you, Judy."

Not that again. "But they could see *you*."

"I'm not enough." Strobe didn't look at me when he said it.

"You're the best."

"He's better." Strobe looked at the stage. We could both see the phantom of Nick still there, leaping, crouching, lying on the floor, singing his heart out.

"But *we're* better."

"*You're* better."

"I'm just the drummer."

142

"You're the best thing we've got."

I wanted to cry and laugh. It was such a wonderful thing for him to say. And it was such a terrible thing for him to say. He thought I was so good—after almost not taking me and then teaching me how to play drums in a band and how to sing my songs, even if I wouldn't sing them from anywhere except my drum pit.

He thought I was the best thing in the band and told me so and made me blush with happiness. But what a weight it was to bear. What a burden. The band had to be saved, and I was the one, he was telling me, who had to save it.

That wasn't my role. I was the drummer. I was supposed to be the girl who sat behind the boys who stood in front of the girls who shrieked their names and wore their faces on T-shirts over their breasts and dreamed their dreams of making love to them.

I didn't want what Strobe was giving me. I didn't want to stick out. I wanted to be what I was, the buried heart that sent life flowing through the body around me, the invisible sister to my new family.

"I'm getting out of here." I headed for the stage.

Strobe didn't try to follow me. He stayed in his seat and called to me, in all his wisdom: "Maybe you need to get him out of your system."

"Maybe I need to get him into my system," I called back. Then I went looking for my date, on this, my wedding night.

42

"Backstage" didn't really mean backstage. It really just meant anywhere that wasn't *onstage.*

For Nick, it meant his dressing room.

His dressing room wasn't like our dressing room. For one thing, he had his own. For another thing, it was enormous and had carpeting on the floor and two sofas and easy chairs and a telephone and a TV set and an enormous bar along one wall and mirrors on the other three.

At the moment, there were two bartenders behind the bar, pouring champagne.

There were dozens of people, filling the room, most of them surrounding Nick, who sat on one of the sofas with his shirt off and a towel still around his neck. Most of the people just stood there above him, looking down, staring, not saying anything. They were afraid to talk. It was as if he were a god.

Not that Nick would have heard them. In the midst of all these people smoking and drinking champagne and trying to pretend that Nick wasn't in the room and life was always just filled with the worship of the sweaty-haired god of rock and roll, Nick sat on his sofa with a girl on one side of him and a boy on the other.

The girl was the same one who had visited the stage with him that afternoon. She had taken up where she'd left off: kissing his neck.

The boy was Mark. Mark The Music. My Mark.

What was Mark doing there? Mark had run away. Mark hated Nick Praetorious. Mark knew that Nick was after me. Mark knew that Nick had done something to me. That he'd opened me up to something. To some possibility. To himself, as rotten and beautiful as he was, some corrupt god of rock who I thought I could win over and make innocent like me.

What Mark was doing there was drinking champagne, which he poured out of a bottle into his own glass and Nick's glass and Nick's girl's glass, which she drank from maybe to cool her kisses on Nick's hot neck.

Nick knew I was there. I knew he knew. But he didn't say anything as I stood there with all those fancy people around me, staring down at my friend Mark and the man who thought he'd lure me out of myself with his talk of making this our wedding night.

He could ignore me, but I couldn't ignore Mark. "What are you doing here?" I asked.

It was only then that Nick looked right at me. "You were the best thing about your band tonight." He gave me a smile that even the dead would warm to. "Judy Valentine, I don't believe you know my friend Christine. Christine, this is Judy Valentine."

She looked at me without taking her lips from

Nick's neck. Whatever pleasure her kissing was bringing her was absent from her eyes. She looked at me the way no woman had ever looked at me before. It made me want to hide my eyes.

"And this is my friend Mark The Music. I think you remember Mark. He came in here very unhappy, looking for a fight, I believe. But now he's settled right in, haven't you, Mark? Mark and I have an understanding. Don't we, Mark?"

Mark raised his glass to me. He drank it down and poured himself another. He raised that one to me too.

"For you," he said.

"No thanks."

He drank it right down.

"What are you doing here, Mark?"

"What are *you* doing here?"

"I didn't come here to see you get drunk," I said.

"And I didn't come here to see you seeing me get drunk." He laughed at that remark. Christine laughed too. She no longer had her lips on Nick's neck. Now she was watching me and Mark. She was rooting for me. That was one way to get rid of me.

"You're getting him drunk," I said to Nick.

"No one ever gets any one drunk. People get themselves drunk. And Mark isn't drunk. Are you, Mark? Mark's just high."

"On what?"

"High on you," said Nick.

"High on you," said Mark.

146

"Come on, Mark." I didn't know what was going on here, but I had to get him away.

Nick put his hand on Mark's arm. "He stays with me."

"Let him go with her," said Christine.

Nick looked at her as if she didn't exist except to be looked at as if she didn't exist.

"I stay with him," said Mark.

"Mark's a great guitarist." Nick raised his glass to Mark. "Your band stinks. But Mark's good. You're good too. I told you that, didn't I? You're good, Judy Valentine. Nobody knows it except for me. But I know it. And Mark—this kid can play the guitar. He just needs the right band to play with."

"What's that supposed to mean?" But I knew.

Nick held out his glass for Mark to pour him more champagne. "Want to play in my band, Mark?"

"What?" Mark looked sober all of a sudden. That took him by surprise. His eyes locked into mine. *Bang.* He didn't mean to need me. He just did.

Nick was oh so cool. "I asked if you want to play in my band."

"Come on, Mark." I put out my hand to him.

He shook his head. "I stay with him."

"Then I'm staying too." I sat down next to Mark.

"Good." Nick raised his glass at me. "I was hoping you'd stay. Mark, get Judy a glass."

Mark looked at Nick and then at me. Nick was ordering Mark with his eyes. I was pleading with him with mine. He didn't know what this guy was doing with him.

"I don't want a drink." Mark had started to get up, so I put my hand on his shoulder to bring him back onto the sofa.

"Well, a toast anyway." Nick raised his glass. He motioned for Mark and Christine to raise theirs. "A toast to Judy Valentine, who is more than she thinks she is and less than she wants to be." He put his champagne to his lips, tilted his head back ever so slightly, and drank off the whole glass. He motioned for Mark and Christine to do the same and then for Mark to pour them all some more.

"To Judy Valentine, who is more beautiful than she thinks she is. Who is more beautiful than she could even imagine she would ever be." They all drank to me, to my beauty.

"To Judy Valentine, who sings better than she'll ever know because she can't listen to herself." They drank to the beauty of my voice, and to my deafness, I guess.

"To Judy Valentine, who makes the spotlights lonely, because they can never find her." He drank another glass. So did they. Mark jumped up to get another bottle.

"To Judy Valentine, the bride of wedding night, from the king of the one-night stands, I offer this toast: Spend it with me."

He didn't drink this time. Instead he held his glass so it just touched his bottom lip, which was still red

148

from the lipstick he wore onstage. His eyes painted me blue, a wild blue with champagne bubbles stinging like needles on the skin of my face.

"Spend what with you?"

"The night." Nick's smile broke out over the rim of his glass.

Christine raised her head from his shoulder. "No!" she shrieked. But at me, not at him.

Nick looked at her with the surprised expression of someone whose dog has just spoken English for the first time.

Then he looked at Mark. "Do you have any objections?"

Poor Mark. He was drunk. The champagne had painted a perpetual smile on his face. But I could read beneath it. He didn't know what to say. He didn't know what to do. This guy was playing hardball, and Mark lived in a world where Whiffle Ball was the most dangerous sport.

"I said, do you have any objections?" Nick's glass was empty, but he didn't hold it out to Mark because he wasn't going to allow him the privilege of filling it.

I had to rescue Mark. So I said, "*I* do."

Nick pretended he didn't understand. "And I do too. I *do*. I *do*. So I guess that makes us man and wife. I guess that makes this our wedding night. I guess that means we can get out of here now." He started to get up. He came toward me out of the sofa, his bare chest and his blue eyes and his wounded mouth.

I reached out my hand and touched him for the first

time, touched his skin, felt the muscles in his chest. I reached out and pushed him back down on the sofa. "I *do* have an objection. That's what I do. I have an objection. I object to spending the night with you. I object to the way you're asking me and the way you're treating these two people here. I wouldn't spend the night with you if you were as wonderful as you think you are. And you're not!"

I thought he'd get angry with me and throw his champagne in my face. But we weren't in a movie. We were in his dressing room after one more triumphant concert in his life and the first terrible failure in ours.

He just said, "Bye-bye," and erased me from his eyes and put his hand behind Christine's neck and forced her face around and kissed her on the lips. She was trying to look at me. She was trying to gloat. But Nick removed her eyes when he kissed her. He made her disappear as a human being.

"Let's get out of here," I said to Mark.

Mark just shook his head at me, as he watched Nick and Christine.

"Come on," I begged him.

Now he looked at me. The smile was still there.

"Spend the night with me," he said.

I couldn't answer that. Poor Mark. He was drunk, and all he could do was imitate Nick. I didn't want to spend the night with him. I didn't want to spend the night with anyone.

I walked away into the crowd of people who would spend the night with Nick if they weren't me.

43

I wandered back to the stage. Only a few footlights were on. Our equipment had been packed away and was waiting to be trucked over the Bay Bridge into San Francisco for our concert the next night.

I found my drums in their slick black cases and popped out the smallest tom, the one with Jeffrey's ashes.

I'd wanted him with me on my first real trip into the world. I'd wanted him with me when I was up there onstage and I was frightened so he could reassure me or I was triumphant so he could share with me.

He was my brother, my kid brother. Who was going to take care of him if I didn't? Who was going to take care of me if he didn't?

I sat down on the stage and put the drum between my legs. I tapped on it with my fingers to wake him up. I played a little bit of the rhythm from the "I miss your crazy ways" chorus of "Brother."

"Jeffrey," I said, rubbing my fingers on the roof over his head, "we really screwed up tonight. I just couldn't do it. I couldn't sing right. I was all hunched over in my seat. You know how I get when I'm really into playing my drums. It's like a dream come true, and then you can't remember the dream when you wake up. Who am I doing it for? Is it for you or for me or for him? You know who him is. Nick Praetorious. He's doing something to me. He's trying to take me away from you. And I know you. All you would say is 'Go ahead, Judy, go with the guy, let him take you away, because when you come back, you can tell me all the wonderful stories of what you did with him.' So maybe I will, Jeffrey. But I don't know what to do about Mark. Mark loves me. I can feel it in him and see it in him every moment. But I don't know how to handle it. I don't know how to let him love me. I don't know how to love him back. Nick Praetorious doesn't love me. He just wants to have me. Do you think I can give myself without giving myself up? I mean, what am I supposed to do, Jeffrey? How is a girl supposed to behave?"

When I heard myself say that, I started to laugh. How is a girl supposed to behave? As if anybody knew. Who did I think Jeffrey was, Dear Abby trapped inside a drum?

"What's so funny?" The voice startled me. I looked at the drum between my legs. I thought, This will be the first time Jeffrey has actually spoken from beyond the grave.

"What's so funny?" came the voice again. I knew that voice. It wasn't Jeffrey's. It was my father's. Not my real father's. My new father's.

I looked out into the vast dark auditorium. "Where are you?"

152

"Here."

"I can't see you."

He lit a match and held it under his face. He looked even more like a ghost than usual. The white streak in his hair a faint flame itself in the darkness around him.

"Did you hear what I said?" I was hoping he hadn't, and I was hoping he had.

Strobe got up from his seat and came toward the stage. "I heard you asking questions. There's nothing wrong with asking questions. As long as you don't expect answers."

He was beside me now. "But I need answers." I wanted to lean against him. But you didn't lean against Strobe. Sometimes he just didn't seem real enough to lean against. He might disappear. He might become part of you.

"To what?"

"Nick Praetorious is after me."

Strobe was unfazed. "That's not a question," he said.

"I think I might want to spend some time with him," I said.

"He's a great performer."

So there we were, standing on the stage where we'd bombed and Nick had burned hot into the minds of ten thousand lovers. Our feet were in his footsteps. The air he'd breathed and sung was pressing on our skin. "But I don't like him. I don't. He's all full of himself

153

and he orders people around and there's something cruel about him and I don't think he wants me except to say he's had me."

"No wonder you're attracted to him," said Strobe without hesitation.

I couldn't believe it. "Is that supposed to be a joke?"

"I don't joke." Which was true. Strobe was the most serious person I'd ever known. Jeffrey would have driven him truly nuts.

"Then what is it with me? With me and Nick? I don't even like him. But I keep thinking of him. I feel pulled toward him. He's got claws and he's digging into me, and I'm letting him."

"He's wrong for you. Women always like men who are wrong for them."

"They do?" But somewhere in me I sensed he was right.

"It's the appeal of disharmony. You know how sometimes we deliberately don't resolve a chord, and we know it drives everybody crazy. But they can't stop listening. They can't let go. They long for resolution, but in the meantime they give themselves over to the terrible chord, they give themselves and give themselves, and that's when we know we've got them in our power."

I knew what he meant. "That's how I feel. I feel like hanging on to him. I think it could tear me apart. But I can't let go. I can't stop listening."

"You'll be destroyed if you don't." At least he

154

looked at me when he said it. But I couldn't tell if it was out of sympathy or disgust.

"Then why don't you stop me, Strobe? Why don't you hold me back?"

He shook his head and started to walk away. "I don't stop people, Judy. It's not my job to stop people. It's my job to start them. I don't believe in stopping people from doing anything. Only myself. I'm the only one I stop from doing anything. And that's hard enough. Like the drugs. It killed me to take them. And it killed me to stop taking them. But I stopped by myself. No one can stop things for you. Or do you want to be my prisoner?"

"I don't want to be *his* prisoner." I felt like crying. It was as if Nick were right there with us, leaping across the stage, coming at me with the snarl I wanted to lick off his face.

"What about Mark?" asked Strobe.

"Nick's got Mark too. He's got Mark eating out of his hand. He's talking about Mark playing in his band. He's getting Mark drunk and he's making Mark do things for him and he's turning Mark against me. You've got to stop him, Strobe."

But Strobe wouldn't budge. "That isn't what I meant when I asked about Mark. I meant what about Mark and you?"

"Mark loves me."

"Mark loves you." Strobe wasn't reassuring me. He was just stating a fact. "Mark is good. That's what I want you to remember. Mark is good."

155

I knew Strobe was right. Mark was good. And Nick was bad. Why couldn't I open my arms to Mark? Why couldn't I stop Nick from invading my thoughts? Was there something wrong with me? Or was there something wrong with love itself?

I couldn't bear to think about it. It was terrible not to want the right thing and to have a terrible desire for the wrong thing.

"Take me home," I said to Strobe.

Without another word, he walked toward the back of the auditorium. I followed him.

I had escaped. But all the way back, I looked for Nick. He wasn't looking for me, or he would have found me.

44

Things didn't go much better for the band when we played San Francisco and then headed north up to Washington and Oregon. It was "Nick, Nick, Nick" everywhere we went.

Most of the local papers didn't bother to mention us at all, because their job was to chronicle the amazing life and the incredible act of Nick Praetorious, but a couple of them said that Wedding Night was the opening act and blamed Entity Records for trying to push a terrible new group on the loyal following of the greatest rock star alive today.

Mitch Sunday began to go crazy. It was as if word had spread that a lousy band was coming to town, and no one would touch us. Rock writers for local papers ignored us, and radio interviews that Mitch or the Entity publicity lady had set up were suddenly canceled.

"We're not copy," Mitch said. We were in a hotel room. We were always in a hotel room. "That's what they're telling me. We're not copy. There isn't anything to say about us. Or there isn't anything good. How do you think I feel to be told by a media guy that he's doing me a favor by killing a story on the band? Look at me, I'm losing my hair over this."

It was true. Mitch Sunday was going bald before our very eyes.

"I lost my hair a long time ago," said Irwin. He turned to Maddox. "Maybe that's why I haven't found a wife."

"I don't want a wife," Mitch replied. He didn't understand when Irwin was joking. Managers weren't big on jokes. They were trying to get rich on other people's talent. So there wasn't much room for humor in their lives.

"Have some of my hair," Maddox said to Mitch.

The way Mitch looked at Maddox's curly black hair made Irwin and Maddox break up.

"Very funny, you guys. But let me tell you something. Lieberman is thinking about calling us in. He knows we're bombing. The record isn't selling. And is it any wonder? Look at the press we're getting. No press or caca press. And Nick, our dear friend Nick, is telling Lieberman to get rid of us. He's telling him to find another opener for him, or just to let him play alone. But Lieberman won't let him play alone, because Nick won't extend the time of his act. You know him. He's got to protect those precious vocal cords of his. And he doesn't believe in overexposure. Ninety minutes is just enough to bring the girls to a boil. Anything over that, and they start to evaporate. But I'm telling you, there's tremendous pressure on me. Tremendous pressure." By this time we were beginning to realize why Mitch was losing his hair. He was running his hands violently through it as he paced from corner to corner of the room.

"There's tremendous pressure on *us*," Strobe told Mitch. "We're up there every night. It's our music. It's our life. For you it's just a business."

"And for Lieberman it's just a business. *The Band Never Dances* isn't dancing out of any record store in the nation. The single isn't getting any air play. We aren't getting any press. And if something doesn't happen, we're going to get bumped off this tour and I'm going to end up living with my mother in New Jersey and the rest of you are going to be playing in subway stations with amps the size of a matchbook. So something has to give around here. We have to get a break, or we're all going to be Greyhounding it back home before we ever get a single picture in *Rolling Stone.*"

"Don't worry about it," said Strobe.

Mitch blew up. "Don't worry about it! If I don't worry about it, who will? I'm the manager of Wedding Night, and it's my job to get you people playing right and doing right so you get paid right. We ain't getting rich off this tour. You know that. We probably won't even break even. But we're not here for money. Money's supposed to come later. We're here for *exposure.* We're here for people to see us for the first time and hear us for the first time, and they'll fall in love with the way we look, so we can make T-shirts for them, and they'll fall in love with the way we sound, so they'll buy our record, and the trades will write us up and *Rolling Stone* will interview us and radio stations will have us on being outrageous and RTV will beg us for an exclusive for our videos and the next time we go on the road we won't be opening for anyone, we'll be the main act and we won't have to stay in a hotel that Nick Praetorious wouldn't use the men's room of and we'll fly first-class, that is until we have our own plane, and we'll be stars, that's what we'll be, *stars*, and the rest of you won't be able to walk down the street without bodyguards and I won't be able to walk down the street because my limo driver wouldn't dream of letting me do it. *That's* what I'm here for. To make you stars. But you aren't playing like stars. You aren't acting like stars. You *aren't* stars. And it's breaking

159

my heart. It's tearing me up inside. It's turning me into a bald guy. And I'm only twenty-eight years old."

Strobe just looked at Mitch and said again, "Don't worry about it."

Mitch was calm now, after his tirade. "Why shouldn't I worry about it?"

"Because we're going to make it."

"How are we going to make it?" Mitch asked, in a contemptuous way, as if it were an impossible task.

"We have our ace in the hole."

"And what might that be?"

"Not what. Who."

"So who?" Mitch was looking around, as if there might actually be an ace in the hole up one of our sleeves.

"Judy." Strobe didn't look at me when he said my name.

Mitch looked at me and shook his head. "What's she going to do, sprinkle her brother's ashes over the audience and make him come to life?"

"That's right," said Strobe.

"What?" I couldn't believe it. How dare they talk about Jeffrey that way? He was mine. He was locked up tight within me. He was inside my drum, inside my music, inside my life. And no one was ever going to take him away from me.

"That's right." Strobe walked toward me. I backed away. I was frightened of him. "It's getting to be time for you to give up the ghost."

45

Strobe told me that I was hiding behind Jeffrey, that I was hiding inside Jeffrey.

"Let him live," he said.

"He's dead." I knew that. I could face up to that. I had always been able to face up to that.

"Let him live," he said again, over and over, whenever we were alone together, in a hotel room or working together on our music.

"How?" I finally asked him. "How?"

"By living yourself."

"I *am* living. What do I look like, a pile of ashes?"

"By living yourself so he can live through you. You know what Jeffrey wanted to be?"

"He wanted to be everything. He was everything. That's why he died. Because there was nothing else for him to be."

"There was one thing." Strobe came close to me and looked into my eyes. I looked back into his, but as usual I didn't feel I could really see him. It was impossible to know what he was thinking. His eyes gave nothing away.

"He was everything," I repeated.

"Wrong. There was one thing he wasn't. And it was

the one thing he most wanted to be. And you know what that is?"

"What?"

"A star."

"Jeffrey *was* a star!" I screamed.

Strobe took my wrists in his hands. "Only to you. Only to you, Judy. Only to you. To the rest of the world he was just a screwed-up kid who didn't know who he was and kept looking for himself in costume changes. He didn't know who he was. What did you say he wrote to you? 'There's no me inside me'? Well, what about you, Judy? Are you going to be just like your brother? Are you going to go on hiding for the rest of your life?"

"So what do I have to do?"

"Become yourself."

What a stupid thing for him to say. Who did he think I was, Barbra Streisand in disguise? "I am myself."

"Become yourself," he repeated. "Find yourself in who you are. Come out from behind the person you think you are. Blossom. Bloom. Grow. Open up. Live."

I wanted to hit him. I wanted to kill him. "Do I look dead to you?"

He shook his head. "Not dead, Judy. Not dead at all. But not alive. Not yet. Not all the way. You've faced death. I know that. Your brother died, and you've kept him alive in yourself all this time. The person you loved most died, and you faced down death and you

162

told it to leave Jeffrey with you, and it did. You faced death and you won. But you haven't faced life. Not yet. You haven't faced life and lived it the way you know you can live it. The way Jeffrey wanted to live it but couldn't. Face life, Judy. Live it. Live."

It was as if Strobe had been looking for a key to open me up, going to the locksmith every day and coming back with the wrong key. So he kept pounding on my door, on me, pounding and pounding and pounding, until now, all of a sudden, he had come back with the right key.

I cried. For the first time since Jeffrey died, since that terrible day in my life when my best and only friend took off for the sky and burned and came snowing back into my life as a handful of ashes, I felt something open up inside me, all my grief and all my happiness destroyed, and I screamed out my pain and confusion.

Strobe did nothing but sit there on his skinny hotel bed and watch me. He didn't open his arms. He didn't offer words of comfort. But he didn't turn away either. He watched me as if he knew I might disappear if he so much as blinked. And while he watched, a wall opened up inside me, it cracked with my wailing, and from behind it flooded everything I was. I could see myself as I'd never seen myself before. I could feel myself being born. I could touch my life for the very first time. And there I was. Judy. The girl inside the girl. Revealed. Visible. Real. Alive.

163

Strobe handed me a tissue from the nightstand beside the bed.

I wiped my eyes of the clear water that had helped to wash away the veil that had hidden me from myself. "I feel so strange."

Strobe nodded. "I know. There's one birth when you're born. There's another when you find yourself. Most people never find themselves. They're afraid to look. Or they're afraid of what they find when they do look. But now you've looked. Now you've seen. How do you feel about who you've found?"

I looked again. I looked with my feelings. I felt my own self. "I love myself," I said. "I think."

Strobe smiled at me. "I love you too."

46

From that moment on, I started to live. And when I started to live, so did the band. It had been my fault, and I hadn't known it. *I* had been holding us back. The drummer, the heart that beats within the body of the band, had been dying because she was afraid to live. But now I was alive. And so were we. Wedding Night got truly married. Wedding Night got married every night.

By the time we had made our way through California and Nevada and had hit Texas, we were really cooking. Our old songs had come together, and I had written some new ones. "Ace in the Hole" was one, about a hidden treasure, namely me. "Against the Grain" was about writing music out of the things that happened to you. "Babe in Arms," my tribute to Chrissie Hynde, my "Brass in Pocket," about a woman who treats men as playthings. "Work Me Over," a kind of Stones song. "The Good, the Bad, and the Beautiful," about Nick and Mark. I also wrote "Troublemaker," about Nick. And "Galway's Soufrière" about me and Mark.

I was singing now, really singing. Not that I left my drums. I still refused to get up and come out front and stand there like an idiot trying to make myself into a lead singer. But I had let the crew build up my platform so people could actually see me, and I spread my drums out a bit, so I could be glimpsed through them, even though this meant I had to adjust the swing of my arms slightly. And I had the mike raised so I had to sing up into it, I had to show my face, I had to bare my neck to the world and let it open me with its eyes, from my chin right down to where my body hit my tiny round stool.

I began to attract a lot of attention. It was natural. I was the only girl in the band. I was the youngest. I wrote most of the songs. I was beginning to sing all my own songs. I was hot stuff, or so they said. I was, believe it or not, the "mystery" in the band, the *mystery*, when here I was for the first time in my life opening up to people, showing my face in public.

And Nick Praetorious told people I was his girl-friend.

I wasn't. I denied I was. But the more I denied it, the more people wanted to talk about it.

We were an item. Even though we didn't exist. Not together.

My feelings toward him hadn't changed. They were still confused. I couldn't stand him as a person, but I wanted him as a man.

The worst part was having to talk about him all the time. It was as if he'd planned it. Now that I was finally getting an interview here and there, and I had what I thought would be a chance to talk about Wedding Night and our songs and my drums and the tour and our record, almost all the questions I got had to do with me and Nick.

The other guys in the band accused him of stealing our thunder. I tended to agree with them.

Nick claimed that the only reason Wedding Night was getting press in the first place was because his name and mine were linked. I tended to agree with him too.

He didn't chase after me any longer. He just kept telling the press that we were a couple. He put our names together constantly. He must have known it was one way to get me to go after him.

I resisted as long as I could. But one hot night, in Corpus Christi, Texas, where he'd told one of the local newspapers that he'd given up all women except for me, I knocked on the door of his dressing room with the article in my hand.

One of his bodyguards opened the door. "It's another groupie, boss," he said when he saw me.

"Send her in," called Nick.

When he saw it was me, he said, "It's about time."

I hadn't seen him in a while. Two bands can play together in a concert and have nothing whatsoever to do with one another. That's how it had developed between Nick Praetorious and Wedding Night. We did our thing, and then he did his. He had never said another word to us since that first night, when he told us we stank.

But now that I was with him again, I could feel his power over me. I didn't want to want him. I didn't want to feel the way I felt. Not about him—I didn't even like the guy—but about wanting to be with him. He was living in my mind. There was a wind in his eyes, on his skin, around his hands, sucking me toward him. I wanted to hold out my hands against the wind. But I wanted the wind to be too strong for me. I wanted to be blown like dust into the air he breathed and the air that touched his impossible body, everywhere.

I waved the article at him. He was sitting in a big chair, with a bottle of beer in one hand and a woman I thought was Christine in the other, so to speak.

"I want you to stop telling the press that I'm your girlfriend."

"You are, aren't you?"

The girl looked at him. She must have thought she was his girlfriend.

He saw her looking at him and said, "Go away, Francine."

She put on a pout and stayed right where she was, until he pushed her off the arm of the chair. She looked at him longingly and didn't go anywhere. Nick nodded to one of his bodyguards, who came over to the girl and pointed her toward the door. She stopped on the way out to adjust the strap on her leotard. She adjusted it down, not up.

Nick was not impressed. He only had eyes for me.

"I thought that was Christine," I said.

Nick laughed. "Christine was California. This is Texas. Francine is Texas."

"So what am I?"

"You can be the world." He spread out his arms. He had on a kind of leotard too, like Keith Richard. His arms were thin, with all the muscles clear. He was made out of ice that never melted, sharp and cold and dangerous. "I mean it. I'm planning a world tour. Why don't you come with me? That band of yours isn't going anywhere. Why don't you come with me? I can show you everything. I can show you things you've never seen. I can show you things you've never dreamed of."

"There's nothing I haven't dreamed of."

He shook his head. "You can't dream of what you don't know."

"I know one thing. I'm not your girlfriend, and I want you to stop telling people that I am."

He patted the big arm of the chair. He wanted me to keep Francine's spot warm. "I'll stop saying it when you start doing it."

I refused to sit down. "Doing what?"

"You don't even know, do you?" He looked around the room. He stood up. "Get out of here. Everybody, get out of here."

People started to head toward the door. There was his personal roadie. One of the Entity publicity women. A bald-headed man who was supposed to be Nick's masseur. And a bunch of others I didn't recognize.

One of his bodyguards said, "I'm going to feel more comfortable if I stay here," but when Nick said, "Yeah, but I'm going to feel very *un*comfortable if you stay here," the guy left.

Nick came toward me. I stood my ground. He got as close to me as he could possibly get without making me disappear and he repeated what he had just said. "You don't even know, do you?"

"Know what?"

He stepped back. He was irritated with me. "I told you you didn't know."

"I didn't say I did."

He grabbed my arm. "Listen, Judy . . ."

"Get your hands off me!" I don't know how I said it. I could feel each one of his fingers through my skin.

He let go. I was vaguely disappointed.

He started to pace around the room.

"I've never met anyone like you," he said.

"Famous last words."

He gave me a smile. "No, I mean it. It's not a line. I don't need lines. You know what it's like to be me?"

"Of course I don't. Do you know what it's like to be me?"

He must not have heard my question. "I'll tell you what it's like to be me. Women keep coming on to me. Men keep coming on to me. I can't walk down the street without somebody coming up to me and telling me they love me. Everybody wants me. Everybody wants a piece of me."

It sounded terrible to me. So I said, "Poor guy."

He nearly leaped at me. "But you don't get it. I love it. I absolutely love it. I wish there were ten of me. Then I could accommodate all the people who want me."

"What's that got to do with me?"

He put his face close to mine. He smelled the same as he had the last time I was this close to him. People always smelled the same. "You don't want me. That's why I said I've never met anyone like you. You don't want me."

So he really didn't know what it was like to be me. "What if I do want you?"

He shook his head. "Don't."

"Why?"

"Because then I won't want you." He smiled his

wicked smile and put his hands on my shoulders. He was going to kiss me.

I knew he had caught me in his trap. That's why he was smiling with such delight.

If I said I wanted him, he would think I wanted him, and he'd have me where he wanted me.

If I said I didn't want him, he'd be able to say he wanted me and he could come after me and I'd never be able to say I hadn't been warned.

"Kiss me," he said.

"No."

"Good. That's just what I wanted you to say."

There was only one way out of this. "Kiss me," I said.

He did, and I bit his lips.

He went on that night without lipstick. His bottom lip was swollen and he displayed it proudly, like Mick Jagger.

That's the story of my first kiss, ever.

47

The next day, Mark told us that Nick had asked him to play a couple of numbers with him.

Irwin said, "But his music isn't complex enough for you, Markie. You'll just be standing there playing rhythm until your left hand falls asleep and your right arm comes off at the elbow. That's a singer's band only. He doesn't need you. He wouldn't know what to do with you."

Maddox said, "Praetorious is just trying to sow dissension in Wedding Night. He *knows* we're better than he is. And he *knows* it's only a matter of time before the world knows it."

"He never even came to hear us after that first night," Mark said. "He told me he couldn't, or he'd lose his insurance policy on his ears."

Maddox turned the color of red clay baking in the sun. "That son of a—"

"His ears!" Irwin exploded in laughter. His hair bounced against his own wonderful ears, which were so sensitive that he went crazy whenever birds sang because he'd keep hearing which ones were sharp and which ones were flat.

Maddox was still upset. "What's so funny?"

Irwin forced himself to stop laughing and said to his best friend, "Oh, I don't know. Why, I think I'll just go and take out an insurance policy on my bald spot."

Maddox cracked a smile. "Why don't you get one on your big belly, while you're at it?"

"It's no joke, you guys," said Mark.

"About his ears?" asked Irwin.

"About me playing with him. He wants me to. He says it'll make my career. He says he'll give me a solo like Michael Jackson gave Eddie Van Halen on 'Beat It.' It's only for a couple of numbers. But I have to rehearse with him. He wants to get it ready by the time the tour hits the East. So I'm going to do it. I just wanted to tell you all about it. It's not like I'm being a traitor or anything. I mean, look at her." Mark pointed at me. "She's his *girlfriend*."

I didn't say anything. Maybe he was right. Maybe I *was* Nick's girlfriend, only I didn't know it.

Or maybe I was Mark's girlfriend, and I didn't know that either.

I had bitten Nick.

All I wanted to do with Mark was not hurt him.

He was in pain. And the pain was caused by me. It seemed it would be the easiest thing in the world to hold him and make it go away. But I couldn't. The wall was still up. I wasn't ready to give myself to anyone. Not Nick. Not Mark. I had broken through to myself. But I wasn't ready to break through to someone else.

What would happen when I did? I was afraid of disappearing. Not into myself again, but into another person. Where did you go when you let your love come out? Far, far away? I didn't want that to happen. I still wanted to stay within myself.

As usual, Strobe came to my rescue. He said to Mark, "Look, I know you've already been rehearsing with him."

Mark was surprised. "You do?"

"And I know you've been drinking with him and his buddies."

"So what?"

"And I know he's let you have one of his girl-friends."

"What?" That was me saying that.

Mark didn't say anything. He just looked at me, proudly.

"But there are two things you don't know," Strobe said to him. "Number one, Judy is not his girlfriend. And number two, the only reason he's doing all of that to you and for you is so that Judy will be his girlfriend."

Mark looked at me. "So are you or aren't you?"

"His girlfriend?"

"Yeah, his girlfriend."

"Sure I am," I said. "And if you don't believe me, ask him how he got his swollen lip."

Mark turned on his heels, grabbed his guitar, and went for the door. "I'm out of here." The door crashed closed like one of my cymbals at the end of "You Always Love the One You Hurt."

"Why did you do that?" asked Irwin.

"You're gonna drive that poor boy crazy," said Maddox.

Strobe walked over to me. He was smiling. "I know why. Tell them."

I did. "The only person's girlfriend I am is me. No one's going to trick me into being his girlfriend. No one's going to win me. This isn't a contest. Judy isn't a prize. Judy is Judy. I don't want men fighting over me. I've got enough of a fight going on inside me over men. *I'm* my girlfriend. Print *that!*"

174

Strobe nodded.

Irwin was the only one who spoke. He put his hands over his large stomach and said, "I love Irwin. Irwin's my boyfriend. But, boy, what I wouldn't give to have two girls fighting over me." He pretended we were reporters. "Print *that!*"

48

But what they all printed was that Nick Praetorious and Mark The Music were fighting to win me.

They said that Nick had asked Mark to play with him so Nick could keep an eye on Mark.

They said that Mark had agreed to play with Nick so Mark could keep an eye on Nick.

Suddenly, the whole world seemed to want to know about me.

Rolling Stone had my picture in Random Notes and said I was the only woman on earth who had been known to turn back the advances of Nick Praetorious.

Spin had my picture and said I was going to leave Wedding Night to play drums with Nick Praetorious.

Foxy had my picture and named me Fool of the Month.

Disc had my picture and Nick's picture and captioned them "Do They or Don't They?"

Ginger had a beautiful picture of Nick, lying down

with a glass of champagne in his hand, and under it it said "Is he moody for Judy?"

Guitar Player ran a feature on Mark The Music, but it talked as much about me as about his guitars. "Does he play for love, or does he just love to play?"

Glam had separate pictures of all three of us, with me in the middle. It said I was revolutionizing rock dress with the simplicity of my outfits and that I was revolutionizing rock life with my refusal to make love to either of the gorgeous men who were determined to peek beneath my threads.

Teen Angel had my picture and named me Lover of the Month.

Interview had an enormous black-and-white picture of me, which took up one of their gigantic pages, and it said that I was the most fascinating newcomer in rock music in a long time, a drummer and composer and lyricist and singer. No Mark. No Nick. Just Judy.

Midnight Review had my picture and said I was secretly married to Nick and to Mark and neither one of them minded.

The only person who minded any of this, aside from me, was Mitch Sunday.

"Don't get me wrong, Judy. I love the attention. This is just what we needed. This is the best kind of publicity you can get. Music is one thing, I grant you that. I mean, without music, you wouldn't be up there on the stage. But *romance.* That's what this business is really about. Romance. Love. Sex. I mean, do you think Fleetwood Mac would have been nearly as big if everybody in the band hadn't been involved with everybody else in the band? Or Led Zeppelin with all their black-magic women? Or Mick Jagger with Marianne Faithful and Bianca and Jerry Hall, to name only a few? The thing is, Judy, you aren't *participating* in this thing. They're only writing *about* you. That's fine, so far as it goes. But I want *you* to talk to them. I want *you* to take part in this. Strobe was right. You *are* our ace in the hole. I've never seen anything like this. Nick Praetorious is in love with you. The only thing that guy's ever been in love with before is his own reflection. And he's in love with the girl drummer from Wedding Night! Amazing. And Mark The Music, the hottest new guitar player in rock music, is in love with you too, and he's in your own band! Except now Nick Praetorious is trying to lure him away. Why? That's what everybody wants to know. And what do you think about all this? That's what everybody wants to know. And are you in love with Nick? Are you in love with Mark? Are you in love with someone else? A complete stranger?"

"Like who?"

Mitch had been doing his usual frantic number, waving his arms as he spoke, pistoning his mouth with his chin. Now he slowed down and thought for a minute. "I don't know like who. Like anybody. It doesn't matter. We're not dealing in reality here. This is fantasy, Judy. Who cares who you're really in love with? That's not the point. The point is—"

"Like you," I said. "Maybe I'm in love with you."

That did it. Mitch started to pull at his hair. "That's all we need! Sure. Just start telling that to the press. You can't be in love with me, Judy. Even if you are, you can't. I'm just your manager. I'm a chubby guy who's losing his hair. I'm not mysterious enough. *That's* what I want from you. *Mystery.* I want you to start talking to the press. Don't just let them report on you. *You* report to them. But don't give yourself away. No one knows what makes you tick, if you don't mind my saying so. I don't mind that. But I want you to be mysterious in public. Not in private. In public. That's who you belong to now. You're a star, Judy. Or you're going to be. Men are in love with you. Women are jealous of you. What more could you ask for?"

"You really want to know?"

Mitch put his hands over his ears. "No, I don't want to know. Just go out there and do it. You can start right now, because there's someone here I want you to meet."

I looked around my hotel room. It was neat enough. All I had in it were my clothes, which I kept in my suitcase, my little tape deck, my picture of Jeffrey, which I kept by the bed, and the drum with Jeffrey's ashes.

I wasn't one of those rock slobs. I didn't tear up my hotel room, throw the TV out the window, and paint the walls with food from room service.

"Who is it?" I asked.

"*People* magazine!" Mitch screamed.

That must have been a cue. Because at that mo-

178

ment, in through the door came a photographer and a reporter.

The photographer came in flashing.

The reporter came in asking.

And by the time they left, I had told them everything. And nothing.

Yes, I said, I was in love with Nick Praetorious. And he was in love with me.

I was also in love with Mark The Music. And he was in love with me.

I was planning to marry both of them, in a single ceremony. The wedding would take place in private at a secret location. Only our bands would attend, and a few friends. But not my friends; I didn't have any friends, only lovers. Of course they would all be there too. We would hand out handkerchiefs to catch their multitudinous tears.

I had started playing drums when my brother gave me one when I was a little girl. He taught me everything I knew about everything.

My brother was a musician too. He played the harp. But he traveled incognito these days. He attended every one of my concerts. But no one would recognize him. No one but me. He wasn't available for photographs.

I loved playing the drums. But I was also a singer. One of these days I was going to come out in front of the band and sing. The reason I didn't do it now was because I had a pact with Nick Praetorious not to show him up. He was afraid that once I started singing solo, Wedding Night would end up the featured act and he'd just be opening for us.

I wrote all my songs myself. No, they weren't about me, they were just about my life. I didn't believe in writing about myself. My life was public. But I was private. I could undress onstage, and no one would know what I looked like. I could pour out my heart in my songs, and no one would know what I was feeling. I could reveal myself completely, and no one would know me.

When the interview was over, I asked the photographer to take more pictures.

Mitch looked at me as if I were crazy. He knew I hated to have my picture taken. But I didn't. Not anymore. I was learning to give myself over to all of this. I was learning that you could go public and remain just as private as you had always been. More private even, because you could create a whole new person for the public, and while they were feasting on the way they thought you were, the real you could walk the world in peace and quiet, still safe inside the new self that everyone wanted to touch and love and destroy by understanding.

The photographer took his camera back out of his bag and set up his tripod. I unbuttoned my blouse and put my hand inside over my heart.

I ran out of the room and came back with one of Mark's top hats. I put it on my head. I smiled. The photographer flashed away. Then I danced around the room with the hat in my hand.

180

I lay down on my bed and got halfway under the sheets. I stared out at the camera as if it were the man I loved and this was the first time we were alone together. The photographer said, "Hold that, that's perfect. Hold that."

I sat on the floor and held my Jeffrey drum between my legs and looked up at the camera like a little girl. I started to cry as I thought of my poor dead brother inside my drum, as light as air, as dry as sand, as far away as the farthest star.

"Take a picture of my drum," I said to the photographer.

I pushed the drum away from me so I wouldn't be in the picture. The camera flashed.

I went over to the drum and lay down with it and held it in my arms. "You finally made it into *People*," I whispered. "You're a star, Jeffrey. A star."

49

The article in *People* caused a real sensation. By the time we hit Florida, everybody was speculating on who I was really in love with. Nobody seemed to doubt that they would be in love with me. But who did I love? Nick Praetorious? Or Mark The Music? And which one would I marry? Or was I really going to marry both of them?

181

People got enraged with that idea. One week *Time* magazine had me in their music column, with the headline WHEN WILL SHE SING SOLO? And the next week I was in their Behavior column, with the headline TRIPLE-RING CEREMONY?

Mitch told me that all over the South, ministers were getting up in their pulpits and saying terrible things about me. "Keep it up, Judy!" he said. "In the world of rock and roll, you know you've made it when they start telling the kids that you're bad. Kids love what's bad. And you're the best bad girl in the land right now."

And everybody was waiting for me to sing. Alone. Out front. My own songs.

They loved my songs. Suddenly, I was the voice of the nation. Suddenly, I was the girl of girls. They were playing my songs on the radio. Everywhere you went, you heard Wedding Night, with me in the background, Strobe out front, our voices blending beautifully, and always Mark's guitar behind us, wrapping itself around my words the way I could never let him wrap himself around me.

Mark was a lost cause. He spent all his time hanging out with Nick, except for when we were onstage. When we hit the mid-Atlantic states, like Virginia and North Carolina, we were staying in the same hotel as Nick and his people. No more cheap motels and hotels for Wedding Night. We were becoming stars. We were selling records. Now we had limos picking us up

182

and dropping us off, and champagne and flowers awaiting us in our rooms. But Mark was never in his room. He hung out in Nick's suite, drinking and partying and letting his beautiful, innocent face rest against the necks of the local girls who flocked toward Nick and Nick handed to Mark as if all those girls lived in a box of chocolates and Nick gave Mark his choice of whichever one he wanted, top or bottom layer.

It was as if they had joined together against me. If one of them couldn't have me, then they didn't want the other one to have me. They locked each other up in their supposed friendship, waiting for the key to open up their prison. And the key was me. I wrote my song "The Key" about them and me. Some of it went like this:

> *You think I am the answer,*
> *You think I hold the key.*
> *You think I am the dancer*
> *Whose steps can set you free.*
>
> *You think I am the room*
> *For which I am the key.*
> *You think I am the womb*
> *In which there's room for three.*
>
> *Well, babies, let me tell you,*
> *My only home's my heart,*
> *And no one enters into it*
> *And tears my life apart.*

I think I am the answer,
I think I hold the key
And if I am the dancer
My dance is danced for me.

Yeah, my dance is danced for me.
My dance is danced for me.

We didn't record it on tour, we just started to play
it in our concerts. But pretty soon people were singing
it along with us. They were screaming out requests
for it and they were actually singing the words along
with us. And that's when we realized that we had
what only a few bands had ever had, like the Grateful
Dead. And that was fans who traveled from one city
to another in order to hear us again and again. So they
sang "The Key" in Michigan and in Ohio and in Wis-
consin. It was girls who loved that song. Girls who
came to our concerts wearing homemade shirts that
said "My Dance Is Danced for Me" and shirts that
had a picture of a heart on them and the words "My
Only Home's My Heart." These girls would watch me
and wait for me as I raised my hands and my sticks
above my head, and the whole band would stop playing after we sang "And if I am the dancer/My dance
is danced for me," and silence would fill the hall or the
stadium, and I'd hold my arms up there, as I sat
on the pedestal that raised me and my drums above
everyone in the place except the sound and light technicians way up in the back and the guys who hung
out on the scaffolding around the stage, and I'd wait

and I'd wait until there was total human silence in the place, until I could hear the hum of the air-conditioning and the buzz of our amps and the breathing of the few people who were still breathing and the blood running through Mark's fingers and the pain cracking his heart and the heartbeats in the hearts of all the girls who were waiting for me to let my arms come down and for my lone voice to call out to every girl who had ever been torn apart by men, "Yeah, my dance is danced for me. My dance is danced for me." How those girls would dance! They'd hop up on their seats and into the aisles and we'd all sing together: "My dance is danced for me. Yeah, my dance is danced for me. Yeah, my dance is danced for me."

I was their hero. Their Judy. They all wanted to be me.

So the only thing left for me to find out was who did I want to be.

50

Strobe knew what I was going through.

"You're becoming a star," he said. "Remember that the nearest star is light years away. You've been shot off the earth, Judy. Stars aren't human beings any longer. You can never be the same. At least not while you're still a star. Of course, most stars disappear, just the way they do in the sky. They either fade out or blow out. Our sun will someday. It's going to die, and this earth with it. The same with you. You'll make the journey back to earth, just the way you're making it away right now. You'll be back. So enjoy the trip . . . in both directions."

He made it sound so lonely. So treacherous. "Will you be with me?" I asked.

"No."

"Make me some tea, Strobe."

We were in his hotel room in Cleveland. Strobe always traveled with one of those electric teapots with the metal heater coil inside. He made his own tea. He didn't use room service, not for anything. He didn't believe in room service, he said. He liked to think his room was his home, and he didn't like men in fancy uniforms coming into his home wheeling a cart with a silver tea service. He also didn't use the maid service.

It was strange to find myself asking him to make me some tea. Ever since he'd told me he loved me, after I'd cried and he'd helped me to start to find myself and to love myself, I'd been very comfortable with him. He was still a great mystery to me, but not a frightening one. I felt I could go to him for anything. He was like a parent who never passed judgment.

"Why won't you be with me?" I asked him as we waited for the water to boil in the little blue pot.

186

"That's a trip you have to make on your own. You're going to be very big, Judy. You don't realize how big. You don't realize what it means. You're going to be very big and very far away. That's what happens to stars. That's why stars are called stars. Everyone can see them, but no one can touch them. And they come out only when the world is dark."

"But what about us? What about the band? It's not just me. It's us. I'm just the drummer. I'm just the girl drummer. I'm a curiosity."

Strobe looked at me as if I were slightly cracked and shook his head. "There's only one wedding night in every marriage."

"I'm too young for that kind of talk."

That made him smile. I loved to make Strobe smile. I was the only one who could. Even Irwin couldn't. Only me.

"There's only one night when everything is new and wonderful. Even if it's painful. And frightening. But after that night, just like the stars, it either begins to fade out or to blow out."

"And you think that's going to happen to us?"

"Every band dies. Or changes personnel. Look at Dire Straits—even the Knopfler brothers split. Look at the bands around the longest. The Stones lost Mick Taylor and got Ron Wood. The Who—Keith Moon died, the band went downhill, and they split. Led Zeppelin—John Bonham died, the band split."

"All the dead drummers," I said.

"All the dead drummers."

"But do you really think Wedding Night is going to break up?"

"I told you. Every band dies. But don't worry about Wedding Night. You *are* Wedding Night. Whatever happens to you happens to us. But we aren't going to survive unless you get out there and sing. It was one thing for us to play lousy back in San Francisco. Those were our first gigs. But now you've raised people's expectations. With your music. With your life. With the mystery of you. You *can't* just sit there behind those drums singing into a mike over your shoulder. I appreciate the fact that you aren't buried in a pit any longer when the only thing anyone could see was the top of your head bouncing up and down. I know it was a major step for you to let us get you up on that platform so the audience could see you at work. I know you've been hiding from the world and you believe artists should be heard and not seen. But all that's changed now, Judy. You have *fans*. You. Not us. You. And if you disappoint your fans, they're going to blame you and turn against you and leave you. It's getting to be time for you to step out front. This is your band now. Wedding Night is your wedding night. Take it."

I couldn't believe what he was saying. "But it's *your* band. *You* started it. Don't you remember? How you advertised? 'Band seeks drummer.' And then how you went everywhere looking for our bass and keyboard and guitar?"

188

"We," said Strobe. "*We* went everywhere. This wasn't my band. This was our band. You and me. But now it's yours. It's yours, and there's nothing you can do about it. There's nothing I could do about it, even if I wanted to. People are coming to see Wedding Night because they're coming to see *you*. Without you, we die. So don't tell me whose band this is. This is your band."

I knew he was right. We all played together, but I was the one getting all the attention. It wasn't just for my playing. It was for the music I'd written. It was for the life I was living.

"I'll try solo," I told him. "But not on everything."

"Of course not. Leave me a *few* numbers."

"I still want to play my drums."

"I want you to play your drums."

"So who's going to be our new drummer when I'm not playing drums?"

"I am."

It would work. I knew Strobe could play the drums. He used to show me things on them in his studio when there were only the two of us in the whole world. He was good. Or good enough. Maybe I could give him a lesson or two. It would work.

I would sing, and he would play the drums. Then he would sing, and I would play the drums.

We would exchange roles. We would share. Neither of us would lose. We'd be backing each other up. We'd be supporting each other. It was like being in a family.

189

I took out my drumsticks. "Let me show you a thing or two."

He took them. "I am honored."

He stood up and motioned for me to do the same. "Now let me show you how to sing," he said.

"But I—"

"This time for keeps."

"I am honored." And I was.

51

That afternoon I went on "Rock Lives" on WMMS. I'd always heard about WMMS, which was supposed to blow out of Cleveland all over the Midwest, down into the South, and even into some powerful receivers in New York. It was the most famous radio station in the world. It was worshiped. Some people called it the voice of God and said it was the only god everyone could agree on, because it spoke in one voice: the voice of rock and roll.

Mitch Sunday had arranged the interview. It wasn't my first, but it was my first big one. The host was a woman named Trish Phillips, who had the most famous radio rock voice since Alison Steele in New York, the Nightbird, whom Jeffrey and I used to listen to. Jeffrey would imitate her and make me want to fly away with him into the darkness of his soul.

First Trish Phillips asked me some boring questions about what it was like to be a girl drummer in a rock band, and what it was like to be the only girl in a rock band, and what it was like to be sixteen and on the road.

Then she started to talk about my fans.

"Did you know that girls are beginning to imitate you?"

"Me?"

"Sure, Judy. Even before Wedding Night arrived in Cleveland, we had reports at the station that all over the city girls were enrolling for drum lessons. Can you believe it? And they're singing your songs. I guess you know that."

"They sometimes sing along with us." I mean, what else could I say? Being interviewed was an art, and I hadn't learned it yet. Mitch and a whole bunch of people from Entity Records were sitting outside the booth, staring at me. Now that we were a hot band, it seemed as if everybody from Entity was following us from city to city, except for Mr. Lieberman, who hadn't said a word to us and had probably moved on to some other new discovery. Mitch wasn't paying attention to the Entity people. He was looking right at me and kept opening his mouth and moving his hand in front of it. He was either checking for bad breath or he was telling me to open up, to say more. But what was there to say?

"It's more than that," said Trish Phillips. "They're singing your songs. They're dressing like you.

191

They're doing their hair like you. They're all trying to become *you*. Have you seen their shirts?"

"Their shirts?"

Trish Phillips looked at me as if I were retarded. "Their shirts. You mean you haven't noticed their shirts? Judy Valentine. There are thousands of girls in the greater Cleveland area wearing shirts that say 'Judy Valentine.' You're maybe the most famous teenager in America right now. Except nobody seems to know very much about you. Why is that?"

"Because I don't know very much about myself, I guess."

Mitch looked through the glass with horror on his face. But it disappeared when, after a moment, Trish Phillips laughed at what I had said. Mitch laughed too. He gave me a thumbs-up sign.

"Well," said Trish Phillips, "our job on the radio is to make you the most known person in existence. So let me start with a question. What is it about your drum?"

"I have lots of drums."

"I mean the drum you always take with you from your gigs. The drum you don't leave with your other drums. The drum you take back to your hotel. The drum that appeared in *People* magazine. What is it with you and that drum?"

"My brother's in it."

Trish Phillips was a famous talker, but that really shut her up. There was some real dead air on "Rock

192

Lives" for a while. In the silence, Mitch looked in at me through the fingers of the hands that were covering his face.

Trish finally regained her composure and tried to make a joke of it. "Your brother must be kind of small."

"He's dead."

"He's what?"

"My brother's dead. His name is Jeffrey. He died when I was thirteen. He was sixteen. He used to be my older brother, but now he's just my kid brother. And he keeps getting younger and younger. I mean, as I get older and older. I knew he wouldn't want to miss this tour for the world, so I took him along with me."

"What did you do, shrink him? Like a shrunken head in Africa, except you shrunk his whole body?"

"It's his ashes in the drum."

"His ashes? Are you serious? His ashes?" She was losing it again.

"I can see them when I play. My skins are transparent. I can see Jeffrey inside my drum, dancing around when I play. He always loved it when I played. He gave me my first drum. I wouldn't be here except for him."

"And he wouldn't be here except for you." She laughed nervously. "But seriously, Judy. I also heard that you sleep with him. With your drum, that is. Is that true? Do you?"

How did she know that? "Who told you?"

Trish Phillips gave me a triumphant smile. "Believe me, I have it firsthand."

Did a maid sneak in there in the middle of the night and spy on me and Jeffrey? "Plenty of people sleep with their instruments. Mark The Music sleeps with Shakespeare."

Trish Phillips nearly swallowed her gum. "Shakespeare has been dead for over a hundred years. So how could he sleep with . . . Oh, I get it. Your brother is dead too. So you and Mark The Music both sleep with dead people. Is that what you're trying to tell me? I mean, why don't you gross me out a little while you're at it? Wow! This is the sickest show I've ever done. I love it. I absolutely love it!"

I let her go on for a while telling everybody how much she loved her own show before I finally explained. "Shakespeare isn't a person. Shakespeare is what Mark calls his guitar."

Trish Phillips gave me a knowing smile. "I don't care if he calls his guitar Ernest Hemingway. What I want to know, Judy, is how *you* know he sleeps with it. Tell us *that.*"

"He told me. And when we all used to live together in Strobe's loft, he would curl up with his guitar and fall asleep. He said he couldn't sleep without it. And I can't sleep without my drum. But how did you know that?"

"*He* told me."

"Who?"

"Him."

"Who?"

Trish Phillips got up from her chair and held out her arms toward the studio door. "Ladies and gentlemen," she shouted toward the microphone, "Nick Praetorious!"

Nick came sauntering into the studio. His huge bodyguards wanted to come in with him, but he snapped his fingers at them and they came to a halt like two buses. Nick had brought two girls with him. I didn't know their names. And one boy. I did know his name. Mark.

Mark stood with the two girls and looked into the studio. He had one arm around one girl and one arm around the other. They each had one arm around him. I could see their hands on either side of his waist. They both had huge rings on their fingers. They both had blond hair. I couldn't tell them apart. I wondered if they had just come from doing a Doublemint commercial.

I also wondered if they were Nick's girls or Mark's girls. Maybe Mark was just keeping them warm until Nick came out of the studio. Or maybe Nick was just using them to distract Mark from me. Or maybe they shared them.

I didn't care. I just wondered what it was like to be one of those girls. They were the meat in the middle of a love sandwich. Girls like that got eaten every day.

Nick looked for a seat next to me. There wasn't one, so he sat on the other side of Trish Phillips.

"This is so exciting," she said to him. "You've never done our show before. What made you change your mind?"

He pointed at me. "She did."

"I know. I know." Trish Phillips could hardly contain herself. "Listen, guys," she said to her huge radio audience, "Nick Praetorious *asked* to be on this show. He practically begged. Didn't you, Nick?"

Nick scowled at her. "The only thing I beg for is to spend my wedding night with Judy Valentine."

Trish Phillips couldn't believe her luck. "Is that a proposal? Are you, Nick Praetorious, proposing marriage to Judy Valentine on this show, on 'Rock Lives'?"

"You don't have to be married to have a wedding night."

Trish Phillips's eyes flashed at him. "Oh, very sexismo! 'You don't have to be married to have a wedding night.' And if you did, Nick, then I'll bet you'd have had about a thousand wives by this time. Right?"

"Wrong. About ten thousand."

Trish Phillips practically fell out of her seat. "You mean you've actually . . . I mean, you've spent *ten thousand* . . . wedding nights with *ten thousand* girls?"

"What else is there to do in Cleveland?"

"You can listen to WMMS," said Trish Phillips, coming to the rescue of her town with a plug. "But is that really true, Nick? Ten thousand wedding nights, so to speak?"

196

"You know how it is." Nick looked over at me as if the very idea would drive me wild with jealousy.

Trish Phillips asked me, "How does it feel when your fiancé—or one of your fiancés, anyway—has had so much experience?"

"Do you have a piece of paper?"

"What?" She shook her head and looked around and finally signaled for one of her engineers to bring her one.

"And a pencil or a pen?"

She signaled again.

Then she said into her microphone, "Nick Praetorious and I are sitting around waiting for Judy Valentine to write something on a piece of paper. Maybe it's her answer to his proposal. Nick has asked her to spend his wedding night with him. It may not be a marriage proposal—he won't go that far yet, at least not on the air—but it's more than the rest of us get. Or at least it's more than ten thousand of us have ever gotten. Right, Nick?"

"Right," he said distractedly. He was looking over at me as I worked on that piece of paper.

When I finished, I put down the pencil and handed the piece of paper around Trish Phillips and into Nick's hand.

"What does it say? What does it say? Read it to us. Read it to the radio audience." Trish Phillips was beside herself. You'd have thought I was Edna St. Vincent Millay.

"It's a bunch of numbers," said Nick.

197

"Numbers?" Trish Phillips grabbed the paper from Nick. "You're right! What do you two have, a number code between you? Come on, Nick. Come on, Judy. Let us in on this. Let all of Cleveland in on this. Let all of *America* in on this. This is WMMS. We send music to the four corners of the known world . . . and to the heart of the unknown. Clue us *in*, young lovers. What do those numbers mean?"

She looked desperately to me for help.

"I just divided ten thousand by three hundred sixty-five. And I discovered that if Nick had ten thousand wedding nights in a *row*, it would still take him twenty-seven point three-nine years. So even if he started having wedding nights when he was only thirteen years old, that would still make him over forty. And I don't spend my wedding nights with men over forty."

"Twenty-seven years!" Trish Phillips was still trying to grasp the enormity of it. "Forty years old! Say it ain't so, Nick."

Nick looked a little upset. "Move over," he ordered Trish Phillips.

"I beg your pardon."

"Come on, move over here. Let me sit there. I want to talk to her."

Trish Phillips did as he said. Everybody seemed to do as Nick Praetorious said. Everybody except me.

But Nick didn't talk to me. He looked straight ahead and spoke into his microphone, addressing the audience out there, America.

198

"This is Nick Praetorious. I'm sitting here next to Judy Valentine, the drummer with Wedding Night. She also writes songs. And sometimes she sings. She's also been getting a lot of press lately. Mostly because of me. There have been rumors about me and Judy. And I just want you all to know that they're true. Judy is in love with me. She keeps denying it. She denies it to everybody. She denies it to the press. She denies it to her band. She denies it to me. She denies it to herself. But Judy Valentine is in love with me. That's all I want to say. Good-bye. Keep rockin'."

He got up. I realized as he did that he let go of my hand. That meant he had been holding on to it while he spoke.

Now there was an empty seat between me and Trish Phillips. She didn't take the time to fill it as she asked, "Well, is it true, Judy? Are you in love with him?"

"Yes," I said.

52

Mark came to my room that night before we left the hotel for our concert.

"Hi, Mark." I was very happy to see him. I had been talking to him in my mind ever since I'd left the radio station.

He didn't say anything to me. He just walked into my room and went over to the bed and stretched out on it. His guitar sliced his body from his shoulder to his hip. He closed his eyes. I thought he was going to fall asleep.

"Are you drunk?" I asked. "Because if you are, then it's not you who's here, and the only person I want to see here is you. So you can leave if you're drunk."

He laughed. From somewhere in his clothes he pulled out a small bottle of cheap wine. He unscrewed the top and took a drink. He didn't offer me one, not from the bottle. But he did let the red wine coat his lips and he offered them to me.

I shook my head.

"Don't drink, Mark. Talk to me, Mark. I know why you're here. Talk to me."

Mark started to play his guitar. He played his way through little pieces of some of my songs and some of Strobe's songs and some of Mark's own songs, which only I knew about, from the early days of Wedding Night, when sometimes it seemed that Mark and I were all alone in the world, the two children of impossible parents who expected us to conquer the world.

It was beautiful playing. It was an old trick of Mark's to do this to me. Instead of talking, he would play, and I would get trapped in the web of his music, and he would wrap me in it until my body lost all its desires and my mind lost its memory, and he would have me where he wanted me, except he couldn't stop playing, and I couldn't stop listening.

But I couldn't let him do that to me now. I couldn't let him do it to himself. We had hidden too long in his music. We had hidden too long from one another.

"Talk to me," I said again. "Talk to me, Mark.

"Stop!" I banged my fist down on the table next to the bed.

He kept right on playing.

"I want to talk to you!"

He played.

Finally, I reached out and put my hand across the strings of his guitar. The music fled up my arm and died.

He threw the guitar off the bed and pulled me down next to him.

His hands were strong from playing. They hurt my arms.

"Kiss me," he said.

I will, I told myself, when he added, "Bite my lip too."

I tried to pull away. "He told you?"

Mark laughed. "He told everybody."

"I'm sorry about him." I wondered if Mark would understand how sorry I was.

"He's my best friend. He said we could share you."

"He's not really your friend. And no one can share me."

"He said we could. But he'd kill me if he knew I was here. Doing this."

"Doing what?"

"Trying to make it with you."

I had to laugh. "This is trying to make it with me?"

Mark looked down at the two of us on the bed, his hands clenching my arms, the rest of us not touching at all. He laughed. I hadn't heard his laugh in what seemed like months.

"I want to make it with you, Judy. I always did."

"I know you did. But where did you learn to talk like that? From those girls you've been hanging around with?"

"Those are some tough chicks."

"I'll bet. Do you like them?"

"Of course I do. They let me do anything I want with them."

"So what do you do?"

"Mostly I play for them. You know me."

"Do they like it?"

Mark stuck his face into the pillow for a moment. He came out looking sad. "They aren't that much into music."

I laughed. "I'll bet."

"Musicians. That's what they're into. They really like musicians. I keep telling them you can't separate the music from the musician. And you know what they say to me?"

"What?"

"They say, 'But you sure can separate the musician from his clothes.' And then that's just what they do. Those girls are so slick they can undress you from

202

across the room. One minute you're standing there in your pants, and the next minute—"

"Get away from Nick," I said.

Mark pushed me away. I almost fell off the side of the bed. *"You* get away from Nick." He took another drink of wine.

"I'm trying."

Mark jumped off the bed. "Sure you are. Sure you are, Judy. So that's why you told everybody in the United States that you're in love with him."

"He tricked me into that."

"You said you love him. I was there. You said you love him. What kind of thing is that to say?"

I swung my legs over and sat on the edge of the bed. "It's true, Mark. I don't know why. It's true. There's something about him. I can't help myself. I don't even like him. I don't like what he's doing to me, and I hate what he's doing to you. He's no good. He's full of himself, strutting around, ordering people around, having his way, like some kind of rock god. He just seduces people. And then he throws them away. You. Me. Anybody. But I can't stay away from him. Not in my mind. I think about him all the time."

Mark picked up his guitar. "And what about me?"

"I don't have to think about you. You're *in* me. You're part of me. He's not. He's outside me. It's much easier to want him. He's there, like an apple in a tree. A rotten apple. But you, I can't even see you most of the time. I see you, and it's like seeing me. It's much harder to love you."

Mark looked confused. Why not? I was confused. He looked as if I'd told him I loved him and I couldn't love him, all in the same breath. Maybe that was true.

"So what are you going to do?" he said.

"There's only one thing I can do. I've known it all along. But I've been too scared to do it. But I've got to. It's the only way I'm going to find out anything about you and me and Nick."

"What?"

"Just promise me one thing, Mark. Promise me you'll understand. This is the only way it's going to work. I'm not doing this to hurt you. But if there's ever going to be anything between you and me— anything else, I mean—then I've got to do this thing."

"What thing?"

"See Nick. Be with Nick. See Nick."

Mark took a drink to wash away the pain. "I'll tell him you said so." He opened the door. "After all, that's what he sent me to get you to do." He closed the door. "See you onstage," he said from far away.

53

The tour was winding down. Only a few more cities. And everybody wanted to jump on the bandwagon, so to speak. Just like that, so fast that we and Entity Records could hardly believe it, we had broken out and were the hottest band of all in the land. The whole tour was now being called the Wedding Night Tour. Not just ours. Nick's as well. It wasn't an official name, like the Virgin Tour or the Monsters of Rock Tour. It was just what they called our show as it moved from city to city, and Wedding Night got better and better, and everybody waited to find out what would happen to me and Nick. When I said I loved him over the air on WMMS, it was like a balloon popping all over the country. Confessions of love came from everywhere: to me, to Nick, and to everybody around us.

Love was contagious.

But did that mean it was a disease?

Maddox caught it first. He had been waiting the whole tour for the groupies to discover him. But when they did, he realized that he was too proud to go off with some girl whose only claim to fame was that she'd gone off with him. So Maddox didn't fool around at all. And then, one night in Rochester, New York, when we were less than ten cities from the end of the tour at Madison Square Garden, and he had given up hope and said he was going to be the only musician in the history of rock who had gone on a nationwide tour and had failed to find a single girl worth his while, he met Lola.

It was Irwin who introduced Lola to Maddox.

Irwin's search for a wife had turned up dozens of contenders but not a single fiancée. He cut a path through women like a shark through a shipwreck. Or

205

was it the other way around? I mean, there was something about Irwin that made women love him. They came looking for him before concerts, after concerts, in our hotels, our limos, our planes, and our buses. There was even an Irwin Kolodny Fan Club founded by someone in Baton Rouge, Louisiana, which had gone national by the time we hit the last leg of our tour. It was made up entirely of women. And it seemed to show up, in its entirety, at every concert we played. Irwin needed more bodyguards than anyone else in the band, even me.

"Why is this happening to you?" Maddox would ask him.

"It's not my looks," said Irwin.

"Then why?"

"It's not my playing. Keyboardists are traditionally the last ones the girls go for."

"Then *why*?"

"It's not my songs. I don't even write songs."

"Then why?"

"I have absolutely no idea, my friend. All I did was tell *US* magazine that my greatest ambition on this tour, aside from helping the band do well, was to find a wife so I could settle down and have kids, especially now that it looked like we were all going to get rich because our record is selling so well and we're the hot new band . . . and what do you know but from that moment on I have so many women after me that I realize there's *no way* I can get married now because no wife would be willing to put up with me, I've

206

turned into such a mean hunk of lover. I mean, Maddox, there's only one girl since that *US* article I haven't been able to have my way with."

Maddox laughed at his friend's newfound exuberance. "What's the matter, she blind?" he said kindly.

"Quite the opposite. She has twenty-twenty vision. And not only can she see me for the fool I am, pretending to try to escape from all those girls chasing me when all I want to do is get caught by each and every one of them, but she also only has eyes for you."

"For me?"

"For you. Her name is Lola. Would you like to meet her?"

"Not particularly. I got enough girls asking me out."

Irwin put his arm around Maddox. "But how many of them have turned *me* down?"

Maddox gave his best friend a really hard looking over. "Turned *you* down? Why that girl must be *truly* crazy."

"Or truly fussy. Really, Maddox, this is the girl for you. I mean it. She even wants to get married and have babies."

"I thought *you* wanted to get married and have babies."

Irwin shook his head. "That was before I discovered girls. To think of it: I was going to make the step from inexperience to marriage without a single stop along the way. What *could* I have been dreaming of?"

"I'll tell you what you were dreaming of. You were dreaming of exactly what I want for myself." Maddox just about had tears in his eyes when he heard himself say what he said.

"Then Lola's what you're dreaming of. Trust me. I know women better than I know my Korg BX-3. And I know you better than I know women. This is the girl for you, Maddox. She's everything I would have wanted in a wife if I had really wanted a wife instead of the boredom of unlimited experience. Trust me. I'm the only person who loves you more than she does. And she hasn't even met you."

So Irwin introduced Maddox to Lola, Maddox fell in love with Lola, and now they were three best friends, because Lola loved Maddox just as much as Maddox loved her, which meant that she ended up loving Irwin just as much as Maddox loved Irwin, because Irwin had introduced the two of them, and Irwin loved Lola just as much as he loved Maddox, not because he knew her as well as he knew Maddox but because he knew his friend wouldn't love anybody as much as he loved Lola without a very good reason, and that was reason enough for Irwin to love Lola.

The three of them became inseparable for the rest of the tour. If you looked closely, you could even see Lola standing at the very edge of the stage during each concert, dancing to the bass line.

In my own love life, I didn't have any friends. The only person I could talk to aside from Jeffrey was myself, and myself didn't know what to tell me to do.

I had told Mark that I was going to see Nick, to be with Nick. But what did that mean? How was I going to go about it?

He was always after me.

He taunted me with other girls, one for each state we toured through, sometimes one for each city. His girls lined up on the runway of his love like the planes that surrounded us as we moved from city to city, waiting to take off, only to land again in another strange place that screamed our names before we'd even played a note to please it. But it didn't work. I wasn't jealous. How can you be jealous when you don't even know what it is you're missing?

He paraded before me with his shirt open and his sash flying dangerously at his waist. He brushed by me so I would smell him, that musky smell of Nick Praetorious that reminded me of the childhood of my life when I'd first met him, those few long months ago, and made me want to throw myself into his arms so he would hold me and protect me from himself. He said my name, softly, whisperingly, when I passed him in a hotel or backstage, Judy, Judy, Judy, like laying claim to me. He looked at me cruelly, coldly, a snake who promised happiness. He pretended I didn't exist by staring at me until I disappeared.

Most of all he played his music for me. I always stayed behind to catch his show. He didn't know it, but he knew it. He sang to me. He danced for me. He leaped and fell and screamed and tossed his hair for

209

me, and inside I went just as crazy for him as all the other girls did outside. They wailed Nick, Nick, Nick, and didn't blink for fear of missing him, missing one beat of his life upon the stage. They cried tears of outrage and devotion. They pulled their blouses out of their pants to cool their skin and let the air of his wild act blow up and down their bodies, until they collapsed and their friends held them up so they wouldn't miss one step he took, away from them or toward them, on the stage they imagined led him right into their empty arms. Not me. I just stood there, quiet and still, going crazy for the man who I knew was doing this all for me, and for them, and for the world forever kissing his feet and biting his scornful lips with soft kisses and promises of nights of love. Wedding nights. One after the other after the other.

He was challenging me. And he was challenging us. Nick knew we were a good band, a great band. But instead of letting us just step into his place as the real headliner of the tour, he raised his act and raised it, getting better and better, because he knew that we were licking at the flames of his music with a fire of our own. And he knew that I was the burning star rising in the night sky of rock and roll that could outshine him.

He wanted me now not just so that he could have his Judy, the little girl he'd found one day beating her drums and telling him she lived in another world and refusing to come into his. He also wanted to stamp me out before I destroyed him.

It wasn't until the tour had hit Springfield, Massachusetts, that he finally made his move. And I made mine.

While we were still in Canada, his manager had come to me and said that Nick wanted me to appear in one of his videos. It was going to be shot in a park in Springfield and Nick needed a female lead. He had written a new song, his first duet.

"This could be your big break," his manager said.

"If I break any more, I'm going to be in pieces." That was how I felt. I was getting so famous I had started to wonder if there was another Judy Valentine.

"Make this thing with Nick and you'll be able to write your own ticket," the manager said.

"To where?"

"Anywhere."

"I'm still searching for here."

The manager laughed. "There is no here."

I laughed back. "Yes there is."

"Where?"

"Here." I touched myself in the middle of my body.

He seemed to get angry with me. "Don't you understand there is no you? What's the matter with you? Haven't you learned anything? This is the road. This is the road to fame and fortune. And you're on it! And anyone who gets on it gets lost. I've been in this business since you were in your mother's body and the only music you heard was your mother's heartbeat. I—"

"How did you know?"

"How did I know what?"

"How did you know I could hear my mother's heartbeat?"

He took my elbow in his hand. "I've heard you play the drums."

This guy was smoother than the guy he worked for. "Are you flattering me?"

"With the truth, sweetheart." He took out a cigarette. That's when I knew he was afraid of me. "So what'll it be? You want to make a video with my boy?"

"What's the song?"

"I don't know. He wrote it for you."

54

That was Nick's move. And mine was to do it with him.

I told Strobe about it. I had thought Strobe would try to stop me. But he didn't. Strobe didn't stop people.

"Just be yourself," he told me. "Remember, it's his song. And you've got to make it yours."

"But it's a duet."

212

"There aren't any duets, Judy. Listen to the great ones. Listen to Louis and Ella. Listen to opera. One person tries to drown out the other one. Not with noise—with brilliance, with beauty. And the great ones end up drowning each other and saving each other at the same time. Remember. No hiding. You've gotta blast that sucker right out of the water. And when he comes up for air, make sure it's your air."

"Mouth to mouth?" I could picture it. It gave me a thrill.

"That's right. When he breathes, let him breathe with your breath."

"I wanna do it, Strobe."

"So do it."

I did it.

We shot the video in a place called Forest Park. There were gullies there, filled with trees and the thick roots of trees and the leaves of a hundred autumns. At the bottom of one of them was a beautiful small lake called Porter Lake, which had a large log cabin that had been used by skaters in the days when it was cold enough for Porter Lake to freeze. It had a huge fireplace at each end.

Nick's song was called "My Only Night with You." It was what Nick called a "dirty ballad." Most of his songs were rockers. That's what he was famous for. But every once in a while he sang a slow song, and most of them were like "My Only Night with You"— cries of desire that drove his fans crazy.

We did some rehearsals before leaving Toronto and then in Niagara Falls, where the tour stopped to rest for a day, and in Glens Falls, New York, and then in a warehouse in the north end of Springfield.

Nick was strangely professional while we were learning his song and being coached by the man who was going to direct the video itself. Nick didn't tease me. He didn't touch me when it wasn't in the script. He didn't treat me like a little girl. He didn't come on to me at all.

By the time we got to Springfield we had the song down pretty well and I was going crazy for him. He had known that was going to happen. I could tell. He had known that if he just got me working with him for hours, singing and being choreographed and sweating and touching on cue and making music together, I would think this was normal life, and this was how it would be with him all the time, and he'd have me.

The video was shot first among the trees over Porter Lake. We were separate. One of us was chasing the other one through the woods. And one of us was running away. Or were we each chasing each other? Were we running toward one another or away? Or both? The director wouldn't even tell us. I never knew where Nick was when I ran. And he never knew where I was. It got more and more frightening, because we filmed into the night, so darkness would fall over us while we were in the woods, and we would be filled with the fear either of being found or of never being found.

Of course we ended up in the log cabin. My drums were set up there, and I played them for the camera. Shots of me at the drums were going to be used throughout the video. That's how my fans knew me. That's how I could keep some distance between me and the man who was chasing me or who I was chasing. Also, it brought the cabin into the whole video. People watching it would know where we were going to end up. They would know we would be alone, in the quaint cottage in the woods, gone from the world, released into freedom.

The cabin was lit by firelight. I entered first, full of relief. I thought I had gotten away. But I was also disappointed. And that's when I sang for the first time some of the words that Nick had been singing throughout the video:

> *This will be my only night with you.*
> *I know it. I know it.*
> *I don't care.*
> *That's how I want it.*
> *This will be my only night with you.*
> *Because that's what love is.*
> *One night. One night.*
> *All of life in one night.*
> *No other way to live.*
> *No other way to love.*
> *Nothing lasts.*
> *We have no past.*
> *No future.*

Only tonight.
Only tonight.
This will be my only night with you.

Then Nick came in. He saw me. I ran away. But the more I ran, the closer I got to him. I don't know how they filmed it that way. The director had just told me to run away from him. I did. But in the actual video, I am running away and yet there he is, always where I'm running.

Finally, just when he's about to grab me in his hands, I stop. And we talk. I loved that idea. The music just stops, except for the beating of my over-dubbed bass drum, and I say to him, "One night?" and he answers, "One night." And I say, "Why?" And he answers, "Because that's what love is." And I ask again, "One night?" And he answers again, growing impatient with me, "One night." And I say, "Then let's make it last a lifetime." And he starts to sing:

It can last a lifetime
But only in our memory.
So give me something
Something to remember you by.
Give me one night.
One night.
My only night with you.
My only night with you.
The last night of my life.

Then I join him, and we sing these words together, except for the last line, which one of us sings, and then the other, and then again, one and the other, one and the other. So you don't know which one of us is living the last night. Which one of us is going to die.

As we sing, we start to make love. I wasn't really prepared for this. We hadn't rehearsed it, not the way Nick did it. He kneeled before me in front of one of the fires, and held my hands in his hands and kissed them, and pulled me down toward him, and kissed my arms, and his kisses reached my neck and into the dress at my shoulders and across my chest and up my neck to my chin and beneath my lips and above them and then he took my mouth on his, in his, and pulled me down with him onto the floor before the fire, where he held me in his arms and I held him in mine and I smelled the smell of the logs in the fireplace and the cold air outside coming off the beautiful lake and the smell of Nick's makeup and of Nick himself, washing me like an artist's paint. I felt myself disappear. I felt Judy leave me like a ghost leaving a corpse. Good-bye, Judy, I thought. Hello life.

Nick took off my clothes. I had on a body stocking under them. It looked like nothing. It felt like nothing. Nick took off his shirt. I could feel the wall of his chest against me.

They were filming in the light of the fireplace, like in that fabulous movie *Barry Lyndon*, where they film only by candlelight. I held him. He held me. We were alone in the world. The cameras, which were on tracks on all sides of us and above us too, were the stars in the sky. Our images passed through them into eternity.

We weren't singing. We weren't supposed to lip-sync during this scene. Our voices were going to cover us in the video. Even now, for the mood, an earlier tape we'd made of the song was playing. We could hear it. We could hide in it. We could drown in it.

We didn't actually do anything. Not that I would have known what to do. But we didn't have to. Our love was in our faces, on our skin. We held each other as our music clothed us. We gave our bodies to each other and to the world.

And then Nick killed me.

> *My only night with you*
> *My only night with you.*
> *The last night of my life.*

55

RTV had that video on heavy rotation by the time the tour got back into New York State, in Uniondale, on Long Island.

It was already the new winner of their Video Vanquish, and it was climbing up the video chart toward Number One. Also, a long version of it had begun to be distributed to the stores. But Mitch Sunday told me it was out of stock everywhere. "People are lining up to buy it," he said.

"Get out." People didn't line up to buy videos. People lined up outside concert halls and stadiums to buy Wedding Night and Nick Praetorious tickets. They didn't line up outside stores.

Wrong.

Mitch took me on a ride in a limousine through some towns on Long Island. There were people lined up outside record stores. And plastered on the windows were posters of me and Nick, lying before a fireplace, our skins a golden red in the firelight.

"Just be glad I got you a good cut of the revenue from that thing." Mitch stroked his hair gently, as if positive things could make it grow back.

"Thanks, Mitch."

He closed the window between us and the chauffeur. "You're going to start to make some real money, Judy," he whispered.

"A penny is real money, Mitch."

"I'm talking *real* money, Judy." He had stopped whispering.

"I don't know what that means."

Mitch laughed. "Hey, I mean *reeeeeeeal* money."

"You mean I'm going to be rich?"

"*Rich* isn't the word. *Rich* is for lawyers. *Rich* is for doctors. I'm talking rock-and-roll money. Rock-and-roll money is unreal, Judy."

"I thought you said it was *reeeeeeeal*, Mitch."

219

He didn't laugh. "You're going to have more money than you know what to do with. You're going to have so much money that it's going to be meaningless. That's why it's going to be unreal. Everything you do is going to make you money. Everything you say is going to make you money. Every note you play is going to make you money, every song you sing, every beat of your drum."

"Money for nothing. Like Dire Straits."

Mitch took my hand. "No, no, no, no, no. Not money for nothing. Money for everything."

I looked at him. His hair had flown up around his bald spot all by itself. "How come you're holding my hand, Mitch?"

"I am?"

"Look."

He looked. "I am. Sorry." He let go of my hand. "It's just that I want to help you. To protect you."

"From what?"

"From money."

"Why do I need to be protected from money?"

"So it doesn't hurt you."

"How could money hurt me?"

"Money hurts, Judy. Money hurts everybody. Take my word for it. Money hurts."

"So what are you going to do, cover me with poverty?"

He didn't laugh at that either. This time he took both my hands. "I want to manage you, Judy."

220

"You already do. You're our manager. You're Wedding Night's manager."

This was the first time a man had held both my hands. Somehow it wasn't the same as a man holding only one hand. It was more like some relative who hasn't seen you since you were a baby and he holds your hands in disbelief that you, like every other human being, have grown up.

"I want to manage you *solo*, Judy."

I took my hands away. "I'm not leaving the band, Mitch."

"See all those people out there, Judy?"

I saw them, dozens of teenagers lined up in front of a record store. They looked like nice kids. They were waiting patiently. "Sure," I said.

"Notice anything about them?"

"They look like nice kids."

"They look like *you*."

I looked again. "They do *not*."

"Look again, Judy. They have your haircut. Not just the girls. The boys too. And what are they wearing?"

"Clothes."

I just couldn't get any more laughs out of Mitch Sunday. "They're wearing Judy Valentine shirts, Judy. They're wearing your name on their knockers, they're—"

"Mitch!"

"—they're wearing your face on their chests. And

221

if you could hear them talking, do you know what you'd hear?"

"What?"

"Your name."

"So?"

Poor Mitch didn't know what to do with his hands. I think he wanted to take my head in them and shake it. "They *love* you, Judy. They *worship* you. They want to look like you. They want to play the drums like you. They want to sing like you. They want to walk like you and talk like you. They want to eat like you and sleep like you and—"

I tried to interrupt, but Mitch waved his hands in front of my face. "Wait, wait, wait, wait. Why do you think all those reporters keep asking you what you eat and do you sleep on your stomach or your back and who are you in love with? Those kids don't just want to be like you. Those kids want to *be* you. They want to be you, Judy. Now what do you say to that?"

I hit the glass and motioned for the driver to take off. "I'll tell you what I say to that, Mitch. I say I don't want a manager. I don't want unreal money. And I don't want to go solo. I'm in Wedding Night. We're a band. All my life I wanted to be in a band. Once I thought I was in a band. With my brother. My dead brother, Jeffrey. He didn't play anything. But we were a band. Together. We were the best band in the world. We played together. Played. We lived together. We shared our life together. And after he died, all I ever wanted was to be in a band. My parents disappeared. When my brother died, they died with him. It wasn't that they loved him more than they loved me. It was just that he took them to the grave with him. But he didn't take me. He just left me all alone. But I didn't die. And I didn't die because I knew that one day I was going to find my band. And I did. And that's why I'm alive. Because I found my band."

Mitch had tears in his eyes. "Wow! Wow, wow, wow! I mean, have you ever thought of becoming an actress too, Judy? It's not unprecedented. Look at Madonna. Look at Rick Springfield. Look at Elvis, for God's sake. Look at—"

"Oh, Mitch." Now I took his hand, just to shut him up.

"Okay, okay, okay. I won't push it. But give it some thought, Judy. That's all I ask. You need a manager. You're a solo act. Whether you want to be or not, you're a solo act. I mean, those kids want to be *you*, Judy. They don't want to be Wedding Night. They don't want to be Mark or Strobe or Maddox or, God help us, Irwin. They want to be *you*. I mean, what do you *say* to that?"

"I want to be me too."

Mitch didn't get it. He hit himself in the middle of his forehead, as if I were an idiot and he was trying to explain the birds and the bees, or maybe just the birds.

"Can I ask you just one more question?" He was whispering again.

"Sure, Mitch."

223

"I thought you told me you didn't even have parents."

"I do."

"You do?"

"Dear parents. But I told you—they disappeared when Jeffrey died."

"They disappeared? So where are they now?"

"Living in the past," I said.

"Do you miss them?"

"Sometimes."

"When?"

"Whenever I realize how far away from them I've grown. Whenever I realize that they don't have the least idea where I am. Whenever I realize that they don't have the least idea of who I am."

"Gee," said Mitch, "my parents don't know who I am either." Then he laughed. "But I guess that's the way everybody feels. We think our parents don't know us, and we resent them for that. But we do everything we can to keep them from knowing us."

"We do?" I asked, and I realized that Mitch might be smarter than he seemed when he was just being our manager and trying to be my manager, solo.

"We do," said Mitch.

Then he signaled to the driver to take us back to the Hamptons, where we were staying in the same mansion the Police had used for the New York part of the Synchronicity Tour.

We zoomed off. As we drove in silence, Mitch kept looking out the window, as if he might catch one more

224

glimpse of all the Judys out there, in search of themselves.

The video was the hottest thing around. It wasn't only selling. Everybody was talking about it too.

It was called the first nude video, although in my body stocking I only looked naked in the firelight and in his arms. A lot of people were upset about it, and they went on television and said I was evil. Some of them sent letters threatening to kill me.

Of course, other people thought I was an angel come to earth, a courageous woman in the body of a sixteen-year-old. Some of them sent letters threatening to take off their clothes at our next concert.

Nick and I were thrown together. Reporters seemed to be able to get us together before Wedding Night's show and after Nick's. Or they found me watching him from the floor of the Nassau Coliseum and photographed me, in rapture. Radio reporters stuck mikes in our faces. And the cameras and the VJs from RTV seemed like permanent fixtures at our shows. RTV owned exclusive rights to our video, and we had turned out to be the biggest draw in their history. They used to announce on the air what times they would be playing "My Only Night with You," and when those times arrived, you would have thought some alien force had swooped down on America and eaten all its teenagers off the streets. Kids would leave their classes and their music lessons and the dinner table and their cars and the arms of their

225

lovers just to get to a TV set. And every time it was played, it would be followed by the latest interview with me and Nick.

He was still playing hard to get. He was still treating me like a gentleman. Everything was very businesslike. Do the interview. Mug for the cameras. Be charming. Pretend he didn't know what all the fuss was about. Ask me if I knew what all the fuss was about. Tell everybody that there wasn't anything between us—everything he used to say about my being in love with him was just for publicity.

His strategy was working. I was dying for him. We were the first great video lovers. Everywhere you went, you saw the two of us, in front of the fire, in the last happy moments of my life.

Truly, I was dying for him.

56

I made my move in Manhattan. Where else?

I was back home. We all were. We were going to headquarter here for our gigs at the Meadowlands in New Jersey and our final concerts at Madison Square Garden. New shows had been added to each venue. The demand for tickets was too great. It was as if people expected me and Nick to perform our video onstage.

226

For old time's sake, our band stayed back at Strobe's loft on Lispenard Street. We could have stayed in any hotel we wanted. We could have had room service send up another hotel. Entity Records would have paid for anything. And they expected to. That's what happened when rock stars were born. The first thing they ate was money.

But we were sick of hotels. We were sick of the road. We were glad to be home. And when Strobe suggested we just all stay in his place, where we were rehearsing, the only one who objected was Mark.

"I want to be in the same hotel as Nick," he said. But I talked him into it.

"I want us all to be together," I said. "This is where we started, Mark. This is where we should end up."

"I hear you're going to leave us. I hear you're going solo."

"Who told you that? Did Mitch tell you that?"

Mark shook his head. "Not Mitch. Nick."

"What did he say?"

"He said you were going solo. He said you were going to be a big star, and you were going to leave the band. He said you were going to tour with him. And the only way I was going to get to come along was if I joined his band."

"And leave Wedding Night?"

"Yeah. Just like you."

"Well, I'm not leaving Wedding Night."

"Bull."

"I'm *not.*"

"*I* am."

I couldn't believe it. I reached out and grabbed his arms, as if he might fly away.

"I *am*," he said. "I'm playing with him at the Garden. We've been rehearsing. I've been learning all his songs. I'm playing with him at the Garden, and then I'm going to record with him, and I'm going on the road with him."

I let go of Mark. I couldn't tell if he was lying. But I knew that if any one of us left the band, there would be no band. Wedding Night was the five of us. Strobe, Mark, Maddox, Irwin, and me. We were a family. If one of us left, he couldn't be replaced by a stranger.

"Just stay with us, Mark. Stay with us here. That's all I ask."

"Where are you going to stay?" He looked at me suspiciously.

I couldn't believe the question. "Where do you think I'm going to stay? Why would I ask you to stay here if I weren't going to stay here myself?"

"At the hotel," he answered.

"Which hotel?"

"At Nick's hotel."

"Is that what he told you?"

Mark smiled. It was a strange smile. It was one of those smiles that's supposed to tell you that beneath it is a secret.

"Don't go silent on me," I said.

"He told me you were going to stay in his hotel." Mark kept his lips closed.

"What else?"

"He told me you were going to stay in his hotel *room.*"

The dream of every girl in America. "This is the only room I'm staying in."

"Do you swear it?"

"Stay here and guard me."

"It's a deal." Mark hugged Shakespeare. He was thinking it was me. He did a little dance. He thought he had Judy back. He thought I was safe.

I made my move in Manhattan. I went to see Nick in his hotel.

It was the usual scene, except there were more people than usual. It was like that in New York. If you were as famous as Nick Praetorious, and you came to this city, everybody else in the city who was famous or thought they were famous or wanted to be famous tried to drop by to see you. They were never any threat to you. They just fed off each other. They tried to out-fame each other and ended up strutting around whatever room they were in and cooing out the sounds of insincerity.

I recognized a lot of the people there. They were actors and singers and dancers and some rock-press honchos and a fat hairdresser wearing huge street pajamas and a young movie star who was sitting on the edge of a sofa and curling her finger at him.

Something strange happened when I walked into the middle of that enormous suite. People started to

229

part the way for me, and they began to whisper my name.

I saw Nick see me and I saw Nick hear my name. He looked surprised. He looked angry, but only for a moment. Then he turned his gaze away from me.

I wanted to go right up to him and take his face in my hands. I wanted to look into his eyes. I wanted to say something to him. But I didn't know what.

I wanted to ask him how dare he tell Mark that I was going to stay in his hotel room.

I wanted to tell him I wanted to get him out of my mind and I needed his help.

I wanted to tell him how much I wanted him and how much I wanted not to want him.

I wanted to ask him how dare he tell Mark that I was going to stay in his hotel room and ask him how dare he think that and ask him to let me stay in his hotel room.

It was terrible to be filled with such thoughts. I wanted what I didn't want and I didn't want what I wanted. I wanted a man I didn't like. I was dying for a man who could kill me, just the way he had killed me in the video of "Just One Night with You." That video wasn't about a real death. That video was about the death of girls who fall in love with killer boys like Nick Praetorious. They wrap you around their finger, and then they close their fist. They stab you with your own desire for them. They take away your life because they make you think you can't live without them. They will do anything to make you fall in love with them, and when you do, they treat you as if you do not exist, because you don't. Your love has killed you. It's the worst possible death.

I felt I was dying and coming alive, at the very same time. There was Nick, slithering into a group of models or dancers or whatever they were. And there was me, being stared at by people, being whispered about.

I knew why he was angry. I knew exactly why.

I walked right over to him. "Allow me to introduce myself," I said. The girls around him giggled nervously.

"We know who you are," a couple of them said.

I held out my hand to Nick. "How do you do? I'm the most famous person in this room."

He finally turned to look at me. "Do I know you?"

Even more of the girls giggled nervously. "Of course you know her," one of them said. "She's in your video."

Nick looked me up and down. "That's funny. I don't recognize her with her clothes on."

"What do you want from me?" I asked.

"Uh-oh," said a couple of his admirers. They walked away.

"What do you want from me?" I said again.

"Why don't you get out of here?" said a tall girl. She took Nick's arm. "Whoever you are. Who is this girl, Nick?"

"You mean you don't recognize her?" He put his arm around the girl. "She's more famous than I am, and you don't recognize her?" he said sarcastically.

"More famous than you? Don't make me laugh. The only person more famous than you is the president. And he can't dance." She laughed. She sounded like a horse in heat.

"Get out of here," he said to her.

"Nick," she said in a wounded little voice.

"Get out of here. I don't even know who you are. Get out of here." He pushed her away.

She gave him a dirty look and walked away, pretending to fix her clothes.

"And you," he said to me. "Come with me." He grabbed my hand. "Come on. Get in here."

He pulled me with him through a door and into another room. He locked the door. It was his bedroom. He had just turned to look at me when someone knocked on the door.

"Boss, are you in there?" It was one of his bodyguards.

"Beat it, Bruno."

"Just checkin', boss."

"Go check your brain at the door. If you can find it."

"I know where the door is, boss."

"Your brain, you idiot!"

"Right, boss." Bruno's footsteps shook the floor.

I laughed. It was funny.

Nick looked at me. He laughed too.

Nick's bedroom was a mess. There were clothes everywhere. Half-empty bottles of champagne were

232

dying on tables where there were bouquets of flowers with notes stuck in the middle of them. Music tapes lay around, quiet, as if he'd listened to each one for a moment before throwing it away.

"This place is a mess," I said.

He looked around as if he'd never been there before. "That's what maids are for."

I pointed to something lying on the floor. "Whose panties are those?"

"How should I know? Or do you put a little name tag in yours?"

"I finally figured it out," I said. "Standing out there in that other room, with all those obnoxious people you were acting so obnoxious to, I finally began to understand."

"What? Did you have some big revelation that every woman in America is in love with me?"

"No. That you're in love with *me*."

His eyes turned dark. He looked as if he wanted to hit me. "I'm not in love with anybody."

"You're in love with me."

He walked away. "That's all I need. 'Nick Praetorious Falls in Love.' I'd lose half my fans. I don't fall in love with people. People fall in love with me."

"I did."

He turned. He was standing all the way across the room. "What?"

"I fell in love with you. Right from the beginning. I didn't want to. But I did."

"I knew it!" he said triumphantly.

233

"You were right."

"Well, you're an idiot. You're just like all the rest. Everybody falls in love with me."

"I know."

He lay down on the bed and put his hands behind his head. He thought he was back in control.

"But you don't fall in love with them," I said. "Just with me. And that's why you've been acting the way you have. Hot one day, cold the next. Trying to take Mark away from me by pretending you're his friend. Promising him a chance to play with your band, a promise you've never kept. Writing a song and a video for us so you can make love to me and kill me in the end. You don't know how to love. That's what I had to figure out about you. I was in love with you. And the only thing you've managed to kill was my love."

He sat up. "You're still in love with me. Admit it. You're still in love with me."

"I was. I'm not anymore."

He jumped off the bed. His black hair danced. He was still beautiful. But his beauty was disappearing from my eyes. It wasn't in me any longer. It was just on him, stuck to him like a curse.

He took my face in his hands. "That's just what I want to hear. *Not* in love with me. That's what I want from you. You were the only one. You're right. I tried everything with you. From the minute I saw you. There was something about you. I couldn't figure you out. That's what I liked. I couldn't figure you out. And I couldn't land you. You know. I couldn't land you."

"Like a fish."

His hands dropped to my shoulders. "Like a fish. Perfect. That's what women are. You put out your line, and they grab your hook, and they shake it for you, baby. And then they die."

"That's disgusting."

He nodded and let go of me. "That's how I live. That's what it's like, little girl. Rock star. Millions of fish in my sea. And they chase me and they chase me in this huge school. And if I don't kill them, then they devour me."

"I never wanted to do that."

He turned his head away. "That's why I loved you."

Now it was I who reached out and touched him. "I know that now."

"Just don't love me," he said. "That's the killer for me. Just don't love me. Because if you love me, I can't love you. And I don't want to stop. I like it. It feels good."

I held his face in my hands. "I feel sorry."

He pulled away. "Don't feel sorry for me."

"I didn't say I felt sorry for you. I just said I feel sorry."

"Then who do you feel sorry for?"

"For everybody. For Christine. For Francine. For all the poor girls you've hurt."

He scoffed. "They wanted me, they had me. You're

the only one who wanted me and didn't have me. That's why you're you and they're them."

"I still feel sorry for them. And for Mark. What about Mark?"

"Forget about Mark. He's a nice kid. He isn't ready for you, though. That's why I took him away. For his own good."

"What a huck, Nick."

"Listen, Mark would do anything for you. He'd even become friends with me, and he hates me. He'd imitate me, and he hates what I am. Mark doesn't know who he is. He's too much like that sainted brother of yours. Throwing himself off the edge of the world. That's what Mark does when he plays. And believe me, he's not playing guitar with my band. He's too wild."

"He's too *good*." I stared him down.

Nick waved his hand in the air to make the truth fly away. But it didn't. "Okay, okay. He *is* too good. He's the best guitar player I've ever heard. That kid can do things on a guitar that no one can do. Not Eddie Van Halen. Not Eric Clapton. Not Stanley Jordan. He's incredible. And if you think I'm going to stick him in the middle of my band up on a stage in front of thousands of people, you're crazy. If I wanted to get shown up by anybody, I'd bring you up onstage and let you sing with me."

I didn't fall for his compliment. "You've been screwing Mark around this whole time."

"What of it? He didn't exactly come knocking on

my door because he thought we could be buddies. He used me to get at you. And I used him the same way. So stop sticking up for him. I'm never going to play with him. He's never going to play with me."

"You're going to break his heart." I felt so bad for Mark.

"Double jeopardy, baby. It was already broken. By *you*. And so, Miss Compassion, is there anyone else you want to tell me you feel sorry for?"

There we were, standing there, the two of us, as I'd imagined it, talking in his room, so close our breath joined as if it were our souls, except it wasn't.

"For us," I said.

He shook his head. "It was never meant to be."

"I know."

"I'm sorry too."

"I believe you." And I did.

"Thanks. Now let's get out of here." He took my hand. "Hey, Judy, I finally got you where I wanted you. I finally got you in my room. I finally got you to myself. And look at me. All I want to do is get away."

"It figures."

"But I never could figure *you* out." He laughed and opened the door. At that instant, he let go of my hand.

We walked out into the school of life.

When I got back to Strobe's that night, I went to my mattress on the floor and took out my drum.

"He can't love people who love him, Jeffrey. What

a curse. It curses them, and it curses him. He made me stop loving him. That's a terrible thing to do. Isn't it, Jeffrey? Isn't it? Just like you. You made me stop loving you too. By dying. You took yourself away from me. You were my best friend. You were my only friend. And you wouldn't let me love you enough to save you. You wouldn't love me enough to stay with me. You let me down, Jeffrey. So did Nick. I loved both of you. And now both of you are gone. Do you hear me, Jeffrey? Gone. Do you hear me?''

But there was no answer. There never was. People who leave you don't have anything left to say to you. All you can hear is your own voice inside your head, pretending to be their voice.

I put my face against the skin of my drum and whispered good-bye. ''Good-bye.''

57

We knew it was the biggest show of our life when Edgar Lieberman invited us to his office. We hadn't heard from him since the last time we were there. Of course, other people from Entity Records had been dogging our heels ever since *The Band Never Dances* had started to sell, and the more it sold, the more Entity people were calling us up or dropping in to see us on the road or sending us little notes in the mail to tell us how terrific we were. As Strobe said, ''It may be lonely at the top, but success certainly does draw a crowd."

"Well," said Mr. Lieberman, "Madison Square Garden. Returning home in triumph. Sold out! And your record's gone gold. That's wonderful. Of course, I have only one regret about it. The record, that is."

"I'm sorry to hear that," said Strobe.

"Oh, no, it's not for you to be sorry. It's for me to be sorry. You see, I'm sorry I told you not to put 'Brother' on the album. And I don't understand why you don't sing it on tour."

"It's too personal," I said.

"But that's just the point. You're *known* for your personal songs, Judy. Do you know what kind of hero you've turned out to be? The girl who can reveal her innermost thoughts, and yet she remains forever a mystery. We get more mail and calls here for you than for anyone else. *Anyone* else. Including that boy of mine whose career you've helped so much." He went over to the wall and pointed at the picture of him and Nick. "What I say is true. Nick has never been more popular than he is now. His record sales are up. The video Judy's done with him is the hottest thing he's ever had. And we have him booked to play to more people in Asia and Australia than any pop star in history."

"When is he going?" I asked.

"Right out of New York. Right away. Nick never stops touring. Never. I think he'd die if he ever stopped moving."

"Like a shark," said Irwin.

Mr. Lieberman laughed. "I suppose you might think of him that way. But maybe this will change your mind. Nick has asked me to ask you if you would mind if he opened for you at the Garden."

"What?" said somebody. Or maybe we all said it.

"On one condition."

"Uh-oh," said Maddox.

Mr. Lieberman waved away any concern with his hand. I noticed his nails were so manicured they flashed like metal finger picks. Hey, Mark, I wanted to say, Mr. Lieberman plays air guitar!

Mr. Lieberman said, "The only condition is that Mark be allowed to play lead guitar with Nick for his set."

I couldn't believe it. I looked at Mark. A huge smile spread over his face. He strummed one hand against his ribs. Then he looked at Strobe, without a smile now. His eyes held a question. But Strobe would never stop him.

"So do it," he said to Mark. It was what he'd said to me about the video with Nick.

Mark looked from Strobe to me. I knew what he was thinking. But he still looked at me as if I had betrayed him, and my betrayal had gotten him everything he wanted except for one thing: me.

"Do it," I said.

"Yeah, man, give it a shot," said Maddox. "Wipe that smirk off his face. Play that sash right off his parachute suit and tie him up in it. Don't worry 'bout

240

us, Mark. We know you aren't leavin'. You're just on loan. Right, compadre?" he asked Irwin.

Irwin was the first person to walk over to Mark. He put his short, thick arm around Mark's long, thin neck. "When I walked out on Carnegie Hall, I walked into the valley of the shadow of life. I mean, I took my chance and I ended up with you, Mark. And with Strobe and Judy and Maddox. But you aren't walking out on us, or away from us. All you're doing is giving us a chance to hear the greatest living rock guitarist play in front of the most exciting audience in the most exciting arena in the world. And we don't have to lift a finger! We're just going to be down there in the audience or behind you backstage, grooving on you. And remember: Nick's *opening* for us. Just consider it a rehearsal. The headliner's coming on next. And the headliner's Wedding Night!"

Mark put his arms around Irwin. "Thanks, man."

"Hear, hear," said Mr. Lieberman, lifting an imaginary champagne glass and tossing a toast toward each of us. "You people are an extraordinary band. And I'm not referring merely to your music. This is a very courageous thing you're doing in giving Mark your blessing. And the fact that you're going to headline after the biggest star in rock and roll opens for you, and at his invitation, I don't think there's ever been anything like this. I mean it, this is going to be the most amazing night in the history of rock music. I mean it, sincerely."

Strobe looked at Mr. Lieberman as if he'd heard

241

this sort of thing before. He probably had. While the rest of us were sucking it in as the absolute truth, Strobe was running it over his teeth. "So maybe you'll finally come to hear us play?" he asked.

Mr. Lieberman knew Strobe had seen through his hype. He turned to his desk and buzzed his secretary to come show us out. "Maybe I will," he said.

"If you don't," said Strobe, "you'll miss the most amazing night in the history of rock music."

"I've heard that one before," said Mr. Lieberman, sending us out the door with the roar of his laughter.

58

When we arrived at the Garden in our limo, there were so many people out on the sidewalks and the streets that I thought maybe they'd had a bomb threat and had locked everybody out.

But Strobe said, "Those are just the people who can't get in."

"There are thousands of them," said Irwin. "Tens of thousands. Maybe we should just get out here and play for these folks. Now *that* would be history."

Maddox looked at him as only Maddox could. "I'm glad our equipment's inside. That's just something you *would* do, man."

"Judy has her drum," said Irwin.

242

It was true. I had my drum, as usual. I always carried Jeffrey to our concerts with me, whether we were in a bus or a van or a limo. And I held him tight against me now. This was our last concert on the tour. And I knew this was Jeffrey's last concert ever. It was time for him to leave me and to meet his fans, and for them to meet him.

"Me and my drum are staying with you guys," I said. "We all play together, or we don't play at all."

"Except for me," said Mark.

"Don't worry," Strobe reassured him. "When you're up there playing with Nick, we'll be with you."

Mark smiled. "And I'll be thinking of all of you too."

"You'll just be *warming up* for us," said Irwin.

"He's right," said Maddox.

Mark liked that idea. He needed to know that we didn't mind. "That's right. I'll save the hot stuff for Wedding Night."

"Don't talk dirty," I said.

Mark's huge black eyes popped open at me. Then he winked at me. And in that wink I saw that Mark had learned something from Nick after all. He had learned how to send a message to a girl. So I winked right back at him.

The other guys laughed.

Mark hugged Shakespeare the way I hugged my drum.

On the way to the stage door we passed by the Seventh Avenue entrance to the Garden. On the flash-

ing marquee it said: TONIGHT. NICK PRAETORIOUS
WITH SPECIAL GUEST STAR MARK THE MUSIC.

"Look!" I shrieked.

They did. Mark ducked his head. Irwin and Maddox
whistled and applauded. Strobe patted Mark's knee.
It was the first time I'd ever seen him touch Mark.
Touching wasn't Strobe's thing.

And then the marquee burst with lights, like shooting stars and exploding comets. TONIGHT! WEDDING
NIGHT!! WITH JUDY VALENTINE!!!!

Now I knew how Mark felt. I wanted to disappear.

But all the guys applauded, so I didn't feel so
guilty.

"You're our star," said Maddox. "You're our main
lady."

"Without you, we'd be an opening act for the rest
of our lives," said Irwin.

Strobe nodded. "Judy Valentine. Daughter of
Frank and Esther Valentine."

"How did you know that?" It was so strange to
hear their names. My parents. I'd tried so hard to
forget them, and not to miss them, but I did. Here I
was, back in New York City, with my name in lights,
and my parents were left behind, because that's
where I'd left them. I looked down at Jeffrey. But he
was dead. And they weren't.

"I've always known," said Strobe. I believed him.

"I wonder if they know about me."

"Maybe they read *Rolling Stone*," said Mark.

244

"I suppose your parents read *Guitar Player* and *Frets*," Maddox said to him.

"I'm an orphan," said Mark.

"You are?" We all said it at the same time, except for Strobe, who just nodded wisely.

So much for Mark's "wonderful" parents. They existed only in his mind. And mine existed everywhere except in my mind.

"I have this." Mark patted his guitar case. "Judy has her drum, and I have Shakespeare. We're both orphans."

I looked at Strobe, whose eyes told me to say something.

"I lied," I said. "You lied, Mark. I lied."

Mark couldn't believe it. "You mean you actually have parents? They aren't dead?"

"They died when Jeffrey died."

"For *real*?"

I shook my head.

"You're so lucky." Mark shook his head. "You're so lucky."

"Maybe you'll meet her parents someday," Strobe said to him.

"Do you think they'd like me?" Mark asked me.

I didn't know what to say. I didn't know my parents at all. But when I looked at Mark, all I could say was "They'd love you." And it was true. I could feel it. "They used to love Jeffrey so much. That's what killed them. So I know they'd love you."

Mark still couldn't believe it. "You mean you actually have parents? Wow, wouldn't it be great if they could hear you play tonight? I mean, every time I play I imagine my parents can hear me. I dream that my music goes to heaven. I know that's stupid. But I dream it. Except you don't have to dream it, Judy. They could be here. They could hear you."

"I wish they could too. But they can't."

Strobe said to me, "Play well enough tonight and maybe they'll be able to hear you."

"Or *loud* enough," said Irwin, who put his hands over the hair over his ears.

That made us all laugh again. Even me. But as I thought of Mark playing for his parents in heaven and my never playing for my parents, who were right here in this city, I was sad. I hugged Jeffrey to me. I was a brother orphan. But I wasn't a parent orphan. Not really. That's only what I'd turned myself into.

"I'll play well enough," I said.

"Then the whole world will hear you," said Strobe.

We were mobbed on the way in, but there seemed to be as many cops as there were fans. They made a phalanx around us and got us into the building without any of us losing any clothes or hair.

All around me, almost pressing against me and literally pressing against the police, were girls in shirts and sweatshirts that had my picture on them.

"Is that you?" said one of the cops.

246

"That's me."

"It must be weird," he said.

"What?"

"To see yourself everyplace you look. Like having mirrors in every room in the world."

"It's a dream come true." Because I was finally able to look at myself and not hide any longer from my own eyes or anyone else's.

The cop looked at me as if I were nuts. "I dream of girls too. But not on shirts."

"Yeah, he dreams of girls without shirts," said another cop.

They both laughed. Then the first cop said to me, "Say, are you in a band?"

"Wedding Night," I said.

"Never heard of it," he said.

The other cop said to him, "That's because you never been married."

They both laughed again. "Let's go, kids," they said to us.

My face might be on the shirts of a million girls, but to most of the world, I was just a child in an unknown band.

59

I went out front to watch Mark play with Nick. Strobe came with me, just like the early days on the tour when the two of us would watch Nick from the audience and marvel at him. Now we were in a special VIP section near the stage. Ushers and guards surrounded us and the rest of the people in there, who looked just like everybody who showed up around Nick after every concert. But most of the seats in the section were empty. Strobe told me that was because such people came only for the headliner.

"Nick knew?"

Strobe nodded. "Nick knew."

The lights went down, the Garden went black, and twenty thousand throats opened up and screamed.

But they didn't scream "Nick, Nick, Nick." They screamed "Judy, Judy, Judy."

"They must think we're opening," I said to Strobe.

He shook his head. "They just want you out there."

"Nick must be peeved."

Strobe disagreed again. "Nick's going to love it. He hasn't had to win over an audience in a very long time. This is a challenge for him. And it's his challenge to us. This is the battle of the bands. He didn't open for us for nothing. Watch."

One spotlight blasted on with a reverberation that could be felt throughout the Garden. And there, at the end of it, like a star at the end of a telescope, was Nick, all alone onstage.

He'd never done that before. Nick had always sent out his band before him, to allow a big buildup while his fans went into a frenzy for him, and finally he'd leap onto the stage and run into the middle of his band, and his roadie would toss him a microphone, and Nick would spin in the air and come down doing the splits and the band would break into his song "Wishbone" and Nick would sing the first line— "Make a wishbone for me, baby, make my every wish come true"—and do the splits again and whatever hall he was playing would be filled with thousands of girls screaming his name and throwing themselves toward the floor trying to do the splits just like Nick. It was his standard opening number, a trademark of his show.

But tonight he stood there alone as the cries and whistles and the sound of my name rained down upon him.

He held up his hand. Since he never talked onstage, and everybody knew it, they all pretty much shut up.

"Judy will be on later. But in the meantime, here's one of her songs."

I couldn't believe it.

"He's got 'em!" said Strobe. He was very impressed.

Nick stood there and sang "The Girl Inside the Girl." At first there was only his voice. Then a bass. Then a rhythm guitar. Then a drum. Then a piano. Then a lead guitar running each word around its strings at the same moment Nick was giving it up from his lips. There was no mistaking that guitar sound.

You still couldn't see Mark or any of the other musicians. But everybody knew his sound. Boys applauded. Girls whispered his name: Mark The Music.

> *'Cause she's the girl,*
> *she's the girl inside the girl,*
> *she's the girl you never find,*
> *not in your heart or in your mind.*

Nick turned the song into a ballad. We had always played it as a rocker, with me singing it from behind my drums, challenging the whole world to try to get me in its grasp in any way—my mind, my body, my feelings.

But Nick made it into a song of loss about the girl, slow, sad, a cry of defeat. It was his answer to everyone who was always asking him about us. It was his way of saying good-bye in public.

He gave them their Judy, and from that moment on they wanted their Nick.

And their Mark. Mark was incredible. He played Nick's music as if it were air and it had been pumped into his guitar and now he was letting it out at his own speed, a bubble here, a hiss of feedback there, but mostly just the clean, hard beauty of the wind blowing music through the trees that held the earth together.

They were like two brothers up there. I couldn't believe it. They fought and they made up, constantly. Nick would challenge Mark, either with his voice or by gesturing for Mark to give, to give more, to play

250

faster, louder, cleaner, harder. And Mark would challenge Nick, taking a phrase that Nick had just sung and winding it through his guitar and having it come out with a voicing that was more beautiful than Nick's, so Nick had to take it back again and try to do something with it that would be immune to Mark's incredible guitar.

It was a hopeless battle. They were brothers in arms. And they ended up in each other's arms when the set was over, sweating and laughing and trying to push each other into the spotlight.

We were all screaming for encores.

Nick came out, but Mark didn't. He let Nick have the stage to himself. But Mark belonged there. With Nick. And Mark belonged with me.

I wanted to stay to watch Nick to the very end, but I knew Strobe and I had to go and embrace Mark back into the band.

"Good-bye, Nick," I whispered toward the stage as an usher pointed a flashlight at my feet.

60

We were in the dressing room waiting for Mark to join us and waiting to go on. It seemed to take forever for them to get Nick's band's equipment off the stage and ours set up.

251

I was going nuts waiting. I was pacing around the room, and when I stopped it was just to beat something out on my Jeffrey drum.

"What's taking them so long?" I said to no one in particular.

Strobe came over to me. "It always takes this long. We just never had to wait before. By this time, we're usually done."

He was right. We had gotten into a rhythm of opening. Now we were headlining. Now it was up to us to close the door on the world for all our fans.

"Where's Mark?" I was worried we'd never get on, and I was worried we'd get on too soon for Mark to join us. He'd been so brilliant with Nick. What if that was Nick's final revenge? What if he'd stolen Mark? Stolen him from Wedding Night? Stolen him from me?

Strobe shook his head. "He's basking in the glory. Give him some time. He's certainly warmed up, isn't he?"

I had to laugh at that. "Let's just hope he has something left."

"That boy is a guitar. There's always something left in a guitar."

"Is that why he calls himself Mark The Music?" I asked.

"You mean you don't know?" Strobe looked disappointed.

"He never told me."

"Me neither."

I started to pace.

"Here she comes again," said Maddox. He and Irwin were looking at photographs of girls that had been sent to Irwin by the New York City chapter of the Irwin Kolodny Fan Club.

Irwin threw a whole bunch of photos into the air. They landed at my feet. "I wish there were just one of them as beautiful as you, Judy."

"Cut it out, you guys."

They loved to tease me. Jeffrey used to be good at it too. Why do girls love guys who make them want to hide? Maybe because they hope those guys will join them in hiding.

"You going to get up and sing tonight, white girl? Or you just gonna sit there behind those drums? This is your big chance, baby. Stand up for those people, and you're gonna be a star for sure." Maddox was rubbing his hands at me.

Irwin came to my defense. "A star? If Judy isn't a star, then the sky is wholly empty."

" 'Wholly empty'? What kind of bull you throwing on my pasture, Irwin?"

Irwin ignored Maddox's question. Instead he took another picture out of his fan club's huge manila envelope and looked at it and did a double take and then gave it a long Kolodny kiss.

Maddox grabbed for it. But Irwin held it against his chest.

"Who is it? Let me see, you devil."

Irwin got up and pretended to run away.

253

"Get back here, you fat piano. God in heaven, you run just like every keyboard player I've ever known. Like you got a piano stool stuck permanently to your flat behind. What you got in there, a board? And who's that girl, for God's sake? She must be something else."

Irwin came back to Maddox. "You'll have to wrest it from me."

Maddox shook his head and waved his arms. " 'Wrest it from me'! Is that English or Wrestling? What language you speaking, Kolod? I mean, who is that woman?"

Irwin put his hand to his forehead and the photograph into his mouth. "It's Lola," he said.

"Lola!" Maddox grabbed at Irwin's mouth.

"Wowa," said Irwin as he started to run away.

Maddox ran after him and Irwin let Maddox catch him. Maddox tore the photograph from Irwin's mouth. He got only half of it.

"This isn't Lola!" he shrieked with relief.

"It isn't?"

"This is the biggest woman I've ever seen in my life." Maddox stared at the photograph with disbelief.

Irwin took the other half of the photograph from his mouth and handed it to Maddox. "Wait until you see the rest of her."

Maddox put the two pieces of the photograph together, took one look, and fell over backward. He was speechless.

254

Irwin joined him on the floor. "That's my entire fan club from Ho-Ho-Kus, New Jersey."

Maddox shook his head. "Well, from what I've seen, it's bigger than your fan club from most other cities."

"And I love her." Irwin grabbed both pieces of the photograph and held them to his heart.

"But you love everybody."

"Never said I didn't." Irwin got up and pulled Maddox to his feet. "That's what I've learned on this tour. There's enough room in my heart for the whole human race. Or at least the female segment."

Maddox pounded his own chest. "Well, there's enough room in this heart for just one woman. Lola. No matter how big she gets." He put his hands on Irwin's shoulders. "And you."

"And you," said Irwin back.

They went back to their chairs and their photographs of all the girls throwing themselves at Irwin's feet—or into his open, endless heart.

I realized they might have been doing their whole wonderful performance for me—to take my mind off what they knew tonight meant for me.

Finally, there was a knocking on the door.

"They're ready for us," I said. Then I panicked. "Where's Mark?"

Strobe went to the door. "They're not ready. And it's not Mark."

He opened the door.

"Hello," he said. "Come in."

Two people came in with him. They were older than the rest of us. The man had on plaid pants and a beige shirt buttoned up to his neck. The woman was either very short or bent over somewhat. She had a pretty face, but it looked as if someone had frightened her once, and the fear had stayed with her long after the danger had passed.

I knew them.

They were Frank and Esther Valentine.

They were my parents.

61

Strobe must have known I wouldn't know what to say. So he spoke first. "I'm Strobe. Thank you for coming."

My parents seemed to find it hard to take their eyes off me. But they did to look at Strobe. They seemed to find him strange. Which I guess he was, with the white shock of hair and the two-toned eyes and the thin body that seemed to be as much a part of the air around as it was of himself, whoever he was. Strobe always seemed on the verge of disappearing, though no one I'd ever met was as present as he was, there when I needed him, in my life and in my mind.

"You don't look the way you sound on the phone," my father said to him.

"Not at all," said my mother, who was agreeing with my father, as usual.

"You mean I sound weird?"

"No, you *look* weird," said my father.

"Very weird," added my mother.

It was exactly what they used to say to Jeffrey, whenever he'd show up in yet another outfit, another identity.

Strobe laughed. I was glad he laughed. Jeffrey never used to laugh when they said that. He would just go out and come back even weirder.

"Aren't you going to say hello to your daughter?" Strobe asked them.

They turned back to me. "Hello, Judy," they said to me.

"Hello, Mom. Hello, Dad."

"I hope you don't mind . . ." my father said, looking around the dressing room, as if they were intruding.

I didn't know if I minded or not. I did mind. And I didn't. I was very glad to see them. And I wished they hadn't come. That was how it was with parents, I imagined. You wanted them in your life and out of your life, at the same time.

"He invited us." My mother looked at Strobe.

"I figured," I said.

"He called us up and said he was sending us tickets to your concert and he left these passes for us." My father pointed to the backstage passes pinned to their clothes: WEDDING NIGHT. WITH THE BAND. BACKSTAGE.

"I'm sorry I didn't tell you I was in New York."

"Don't be silly," said my mother. "We knew you were in New York. We've known where you were the whole tour."

"That's right," said my father. "We knew when you were in Seattle and Spokane and Medford and Reno and Oakland and San Francisco and Fresno and Bakersfield and—"

"That's enough, Frank." My mother put her hand on his arm. Then she said to me, "Your father memorized your entire schedule."

I couldn't believe it. "But how did you—?"

"Oh," said my mother, "we read *Rolling Stone* and *Billboard* and *Trouser Press* and *Glam* and *New York Rocker* and *Spin* and *Circus* and *Disc* and *Flexi-Pop* and *Midnight Revue* and *The Face* and *Teen Angel* and *Bravo* and *Ginger* and *Smash Hits* and *Zig Zag* and *Foxy*—I mean, the nerve of them, Judy, to name you Fool of the Month!—and *Cashbox* and *Musician.* And we got copies of all the local papers where you were playing. That's why we're so grateful to Strobe here. We wanted to hear you so much, but we weren't sure . . ." She stopped and looked at my father for help.

"We weren't sure you wanted us here," he said.

"But I told them you did," said Strobe. "I told them that you finally had your act down and that this was the night you were going to step out from behind your drums and that of all the people in the world, they were the ones you most wanted to see you and hear you."

258

"Except for your brother, of course," said my father.

"Your brother," added my mother.

They never said his name. They hadn't since the day he'd died.

"Poor Jeffrey," I said. Tears came to my eyes. "Poor Jeffrey."

"We miss him so," said my father.

"And we miss you too," said my mother.

I wanted to run away. But there was nowhere to go. I'd been everywhere anyway. And I hadn't escaped from anyone. Not from them. Not from Jeffrey. Not from myself.

I had missed them. But I'd missed myself more, a young girl with real and alive parents who had tried to pretend she didn't have any parents because maybe then she wouldn't have to face the people who were the saddest of all because their son had died. And if she didn't have any parents, then maybe that meant their son hadn't really died and she could somehow keep him alive. But she couldn't. He was dead, and his ashes were in her drum. They were alive, and they were standing within her reach.

I held my arms open. As they came into them, and they put their arms around me, I realized something else. "I did miss you," I cried. "I did. I missed you. I did miss you."

Applause came from across the room. It was Irwin and Maddox, who were hugging each other just the way my parents and I were hugging.

Strobe stood next to us, nodding. He knew. He had known all along. But he had known even more than I thought.

"I'm sorry I ran away," I said to my parents, holding their heads against mine so they wouldn't be able to see me like this. "I'm sorry I moved out without telling you and you didn't know where I was and—"

My mother took my face in her hands and looked into it. My father put his arm around her shoulder. "Oh, we knew where you were. We always knew where you were. We knew you were at his place. At Strobe's. We knew you went off to find your band. And we knew when you found it. Wedding Night. We knew all about it."

"But how—?"

They looked from me to Strobe.

And then I knew.

"You *told* them," I said to him.

Strobe nodded.

"The whole time I was with you, they knew I was with you, because you told them."

"Yes."

"But how?"

"Have you ever heard of the telephone?"

I laughed. I couldn't help it. "But why?"

"Because they're your parents. And they cared about you. And I wanted them to know where you were even if you didn't."

"But why didn't you tell me?"

"Because you didn't want to know. You wanted to

live in your own world. The Judy world. That's what I called it to myself. The world where there was music all the time and there was a band for you to play in and your brother was alive because you kept him alive, just the way he's alive now, in your heart, and in their hearts, and just the way there's music all the time, and just the way there's a band for you to play in. Except now your parents are in your world. They're back in your world. And there's still music. And there's us. Your band."

At that moment the door opened, and the rest of the band walked in. It was Mark. He had a towel around his neck, Shakespeare against his body, and a huge smile on his face. I knew it had been there since his glorious set with Nick.

He looked at me. He looked at Strobe. He looked at Frank and Esther Valentine. He recognized them immediately. He must have seen me in them.

"Your parents!" He practically ran over to us. "Hi! How are you? I'm—"

"Mark," said my father.

"Mark The Music," said my mother.

"We've read all about you," said my father.

"And there's something I've always wanted to ask you."

"So ask me," he said.

"Well, I just wanted to know where you got your name." My mother was looking up and down as she spoke. I knew she was thinking about Jeffrey. But her face wasn't mournful. She was smiling. "I mean,

261

it *is* a strange name. And my husband and I were just wondering. . . ."

"It's the name I want," said Mark. "That's all. It's the name I want."

"I wish I had the name I want," said my father. "I mean, if you think I want to be Francis . . ."

"So, how about Esther?" said my mother. "It always made me feel like some old lady from the Bible."

Then they both looked at me.

I smiled at them. "I've always loved being Judy."

"And we've always loved you being Judy," said my father.

"Judy," said my mother.

There was a knock at the door. "Time," said a voice.

"We're on," said Strobe. He turned to my parents. "It's been a pleasure, Mr. and Mrs. Valentine. Nice to have met you at last."

"The pleasure is all ours," said my father.

"And we thank you from the bottom of our hearts," said my mother.

"After you," said Strobe.

With my parents leading the way, Wedding Night went out to conquer New York.

62

I was nervous at first. The Garden was so huge. The only other time I'd stood on that stage, that afternoon, it had been for a sound check. I'd been able to see all around me the empty red and green and blue seats, stretching up to the retired numbers of a bunch of Knicks and one Ranger, numbers that hung like tombstones from the rafters.

But now every seat was filled. I could even see my own face staring back at me, huge from sweatshirts on girls and boys. It used to be that giant Frankie Goes to Hollywood RELAX. Now it was the face of Judy Valentine printed around the front and back of shirts like a chain wrapping everybody in their own fame. Or obscurity. What was the difference? Fame was just an exaggerated form of obscurity. The more famous you got, the more people there were who didn't know who you really were.

But they certainly knew my name. "Judy, Judy, Judy," they chanted, as we waited in the darkness at the lip of the stage to be announced. "Judy, Judy, Judy."

I shrugged my shoulders. I was embarrassed in front of the other guys. But Irwin patted me on the back. "Believe me," he said, "they'd scream my name if it didn't sound so ridiculous. 'Irwin, Irwin, Irwin.' I mean, your name just lends itself to screaming, Judy. I know I'd scream it if I were out there." And then he whispered in my ear, "Judy, Judy, Judy."

"Thanks, Irwin," I said, just as the voice of a famous disc jockey from Lake Success, New York, said over the PA system, "Ladies and gentlemen, here they are, the hottest band in the land, headlining for the first time in their brief but brilliant career. It's Irwin the K, Mad Maddox, the Thin Man AKA Strobe, Mark The Beautiful Music, and the newest, biggest star in the land, the girl behind the girl, Judy Valentine! Make every night your wedding night. Let's give a New York welcome to New York's own WEDDING NIGHT!"

We ran out and tried to trample that idiot on the way. "Watch out for Mad Maddox," said Maddox, who held hands with Irwin as they rushed across the stage in the flashlight beams and nearly clotheslined the guy.

I got a push from a couple of roadies up onto the first platform on the way to my drums. I'd never played up this high before. It was like being on a mountain. No more pit. No more little head sticking out with a cymbal for a hat. I was up there where drummers belonged, in the power station.

We kicked off with one of Strobe's songs, "Woman from Mars." Strobe soloed on the vocal, and you could actually picture him with his arm around a woman, a woman from Mars, who looked remarkably like Strobe himself.

Then we played one of my things and a blues number by Maddox and a song by Irwin called "Carnegie Hall," which was going to be on our next album. We didn't play anything by Mark, because Mark was the only one of us who didn't write his songs down. Mark just played. His compositions came right out of his guitar.

After that, we really began to get into my songs. I was still up there behind the drums, singing "Babe in Arms" and "Against the Grain" and "Alone (Alone Again)" and "Your Place or Mine?" and "Ace in the Hole." Then I took a break from solo work and we all sang "Work Me Over" and "The Band Never Dances," which we had to play for over seventeen minutes, because it was the title song from our album and our biggest rocker and dance number, and as we went on more and more people got up and danced, and they didn't want to stop and wouldn't let us stop and they made the Garden shake, literally, they made the Garden shake.

After that, Strobe said into the microphone, "We're going to take a break," and everybody booed, but I knew Strobe didn't mean it, because opening acts never took a break, and we certainly weren't going to take one now for the first time we were headlining. "Cut the lights!" Strobe screamed, and he waved his hands way up toward where the lighting engineers lived, somewhere near the sun.

The stage went black. I sat way up there on my throne and used the opportunity to pull a towel from behind my seat and dry off. Dim houselights were on, so I could see thousands of people sitting and standing there, whispering, wondering. I could make out my face a thousand times.

I saw a flashlight come toward me. It was one of our roadies, with Strobe.

He put one hand on my hand. Then he wrapped it around my sticks.

"My turn," he said. "Your turn. Get down there."

I gave my drums to Strobe. All but my Jeffrey drum, which I carried down with me.

As I walked in the darkness, Strobe beat out a rhythm on the bass drum. It was like hearing my mother's heart when I was being born. Or my own heart now, frightened and excited.

Maddox and Irwin were standing together, waiting for me. They patted me on the behind as I went past.

Mark whispered "I'm with you" as I went by him. Or I thought he did. Maybe it was his guitar that talked.

I put the Jeffrey drum behind me, grabbed a mike, and *bang* was shot with a light that glued me to the stage and brought me and the world to life.

And I began to sing:

> *Everybody wants her,*
> *everybody needs her,*
> *everybody wants to grab a piece*
> *of her life.*
> *But nobody gets her,*
> *and nobody knows her,*
> *and nobody's ever gonna*
> *call her his wife.*

'Cause she's the girl,
she's the girl inside the girl,
she's the girl you never find,
not in your heart or in your mind.

It was what they wanted. Over and over again, they made me take the chorus, and every time they would sing it along with me. They were me. I was them.

They loved me, and I loved them. It was real, even if it would be over when the music stopped or when someone else came along and they forgot my songs or when my face and my name finally disappeared into their washing machines. But for now, at this moment, it was our wedding night, me and these people, me and these strangers, me and the world. I *gave* myself. I opened up and gave myself. That's what life was. I married the people I loved and who loved me, and it felt so good.

I sang songs for the men in my life. "Trouble-maker" for Nick.

You were always making trouble,
It was like that from the start,
You were always making trouble,
Making trouble in my heart.

"Galway's Soufrière" for Mark.

We walked upon the mountain,
The earth breathed on our skin,
You opened up your arms for me,
But I could not come in.

267

I'm like a young volcano,
My passions held within,
But on the last day of the earth
I'll open up and let you in.

Oh fire, fire, fire,
It burns my love and me,
But it makes us too hot to touch
Except we do, except we do, except we do. . . .
We burn each other up.

And I sang "The Good, the Bad, and the Beautiful,"
for both of them. Girls always loved that song. They
loved to sing along with it. They loved to be able to
say:

I love men
And men love me
I love the good, bad, and ugly,
But of all the men
the two I love best,
are the beautiful men
who can pass my test.

I never tell what the test is. That's the good part.
If you leave things to a woman's imagination, the
things she'll imagine will surpass all visions of paradise.

Mark was getting closer and closer to me as we
went through the songs, and staying longer and longer at my side. He was playing as beautifully as ever.

Mark never had off nights, not as a musician. He saved all those for his human life. When he played music, it was only a question of how good he would be that night.

Tonight he just moved on from how he'd played with Nick. Tonight his music was being recorded in the sky, like the Big Bang that Jeffrey once told me about, the huge crash at the moment of the creation of the universe, which some scientists had recorded as it still reverberated through space and time, to this very day, billions of years later.

That's what Mark's playing was like tonight. It would be heard in fifteen billion years, and no matter what people then were doing, they would stop to rock with Mark The Music.

"You're fabulous," he whispered to me in the middle of one of his solos, when his shoulder was touching mine and I could smell his hair. I'd never smelled him before. But it was Mark. I could have closed my eyes and known. It was sweet, sweet Mark, the boy within the boy.

"There's someone I want you to meet," he said when that number was over.

That's all I needed. Some stranger coming on in the middle of our act.

"Who?"

Mark waved toward the wings. He waved and waved and waved again. The audience saw him, and they started to wave. I imagined a cool wind blowing over all of us, roasting on the stage. But what I got was a hot fellow who finally leaped out of the wings and ran to me and Mark.

It was Nick. The place went wild. He said, "I hope I'm not interrupting anything," and we all laughed.

"You were great tonight, man," he said to Mark. "And you," he said to me, "you . . ."

"Tell her," said Mark.

Nick shook his head. He motioned toward a roadie and put his hand to his mouth. The roadie threw him a microphone. "Let's do it," he said.

"Do what?"

Nick smiled and started to sing.

> *This will be my only night with you.*
> *I know it. I know it.*
> *I don't care.*
> *That's how I want it.*
> *This will be my only night with you.*

And I sang:

> *Because that's what love is.*
> *One night. One night.*
> *All of life in one night.*

And together we sang:

> *No other way to live.*
> *No other way to love.*
> *Nothing lasts.*
> *We have no past.*

270

No future.
Only tonight.
Only tonight.
This will be my only night with you.

At the end of the song, though, we didn't sing "The last night of my life." We sang "The last night of my life with you."

And it was. We were together during that song the way we'd never been before, not in the video, not in his hotel room, not even in my mind. I held him, and he held me, on the last night of our life together.

He ran off the stage just as we finished and had hugged for one last time. He left me to all the glory, all the people who were going absolutely crazy for the two of us together and were rushing the stage or standing on their seats, pumping their arms in the air, crying into their sleeves, calling our names together.

And he didn't come back for a bow.

He was gone. I knew it. Our last show, the end of the tour, and he was gone while I was captured on the stage.

I wanted him gone. And I wanted to run after him.

But he was gone. And I was here, with my band, with my life in my hands.

The place got quiet. It was strange. It was as if people knew what I was going through.

I picked up my Jeffrey drum. I held it to my body as I walked to the very edge of the stage.

"He's gone, Jeffrey," I said.

No answer.

I looked up and spoke into the mike. "I want to dedicate this song to my parents. I'm glad I have them. And I'm glad they had me." People laughed and applauded. They went on applauding until I finally held up my hands and started to sing "Brother."

I didn't think of my parents as I sang it. I thought only of Jeffrey.

Come back, come back, come back to life,
I miss your crazy ways,
Come back, come back, come back to life,
And I'll be sure it stays
The kind of life you want it to be,
The kind of life you want to live with me. . . .

Oh, brother, brother!
Listen to your sister.
She wants you to come back to life
And tell her that you miss her.

And when it was all over, I banged my Jeffrey drum for the last time and put my fingers into the skin, dug them through until I thought they might come off in my hand, and ripped open the skin.

"Play, Mark," I called to him. "Play like the wind."

Mark began to play the same melody he had first played for me and Strobe that day in Central Park.

He played while I turned the drum upside down and let the ashes fall.

272

He played so the ashes blew off the stage and flew out over the huge crowd and settled in among them, touching them all, entering their lives.

"Play your silent harp for all these people, Jeffrey. Play for your fans, my long-lost brother. My forgotten love. My hero."

Jeffrey was gone. Long live Jeffrey.

I turned back to the band and walked toward Mark, opening my arms.

Epilogue

We took a break after the concert. Our tour was over. We were more tired than we had realized. And we needed some time away from one another.

So we took a day off.

The day after that, we were right back in Strobe's loft, coming up with some new songs for our next album.

Our first album, *The Band Never Dances*, went platinum not long after the Madison Square Garden concert, and Entity Records said that if we didn't get started on a new album soon, for release the next year with a backup tour that would make our first tour look like a trip to the corner drugstore, then we wouldn't get rich enough to match our fame, and there was nothing more pitiful, an Entity A&R man told us, than famous people without famous bucks.

But that isn't why we went right back to rehearsals and composition. We did because we were bursting with new music. And because we didn't want to be away from one another. The band was our life. The band was our home.

Not that we all lived there.

Maddox went off to live with Lola. Pretty soon he sent us an invitation asking if we would play at their wedding. We did, and the bridegroom joined us on bass. Irwin was best man. He didn't know who to bring so he ended up with six dates, all regional directors of the Irwin Kolodny Fan Club who had flown in just for the occasion. Irwin made a speech at the reception and wished Maddox and Lola a happy and fruitful life. Little did he know that nine months later there would be a beautiful piece of fruit, boy fruit, and that he would be named Irwin.

Mitch Sunday was at the wedding too. The most miraculous thing had happened to him. Right after the tour, and after our triumph at Madison Square Garden, his hair had started to grow back. He was so proud of it that he had not cut it since. Because it was curly hair, it wasn't growing down but out. Mitch looked like a huge sunflower. And he was just as joyful.

He still wanted to be my manager. But I said I

274

didn't need one. I wasn't a solo act. I had been alone before. I had been alone from the time Jeffrey died until I found Strobe. And together we had found our band.

"But you could be the biggest thing in America," Mitch said. "You could make Madonna look like a figurine on someone's dashboard. And I can help you, Judy."

"Just help me remember the words to my songs, Mitch."

"I'm a manager, not a prompter." Mitch was pretending to be insulted. But he finally gave up. "Okay," he said. "You got a deal." And he began to sing: "Alone, alone again, I don't like women and I'm through with men. . . ."

Edgar Lieberman invited me to his office one day. He said he wanted to show me something and tell me something.

"What about the rest of the band?" I asked.

"Just you, Judy."

When I got there, he put his arm around my shoulder and walked me over toward the wall.

"Look," he said.

There was a picture of him and me. It had been taken in the Madison Square Garden dressing room after the concert. In the picture, Mr. Lieberman was looking down at me as if I had come to save the world and he was the first in line for salvation.

He had hung the picture right next to the one of

him and Nick. He pointed to it. "And that's what I wanted to tell you," he said. "Nick is in Singapore right now. His tour is an enormous hit. We've extended it. He's going to be out for over a year and a half. He's going to play for more people in a shorter amount of time than any other musician in history. He's going to practically every country in the world except South Africa. And do you know why?"

I shook my head. But I said, "So he can get a lot of frequent flier miles?"

Mr. Lieberman laughed. He put his hand on my head. "No, Judy. The reason he's out for so long is so he can be as far away from you as possible for as long as possible. He's afraid of you, Judy. He doesn't want to want you. Do you know, he called me from Singapore the day before yesterday. He asked me to give you a message. Would you like to know what it is?"

I didn't want to want to know. But I did want to know. So I said, "Yes and no."

"Let me deal solely with the yes part of that if I may. Here's what Nick said. He said, 'Tell Judy to tell Mark to take good care of her.' "

"Oh, Mr. Lieberman." I didn't know what came over me. I threw myself into his arms.

He wasn't the world's biggest hugger. He was one of those people who thinks that no embrace is complete unless he's patting you on the back, and not with one hand but with both. I would have asked him if he was trying to burp me, if he hadn't been Mr. Lieberman.

I used to go to visit Strobe a lot in his loft. So did my parents. He became good friends with them.

"They want you to keep living with them," he said one day. He knew I was planning to move out. "They want you to live at home."

"My only home's my heart."

"That's what I told them you'd say."

"You know me too well."

Strobe shook his head. "I know you about as well as you know me."

"That reminds me of something. There are a few things I'd like to ask you, Strobe. For example—"

He held up his hand.

"Come on," I said. "Give me a break. All I want to know is who you are. I mean, what were you born as? Not Strobe. I know that. So who are you? Why do you have so many names?"

"I was a session musician," he said. "I sang backup vocals. I was nameless. I was faceless. Everywhere I went I was someone else. I was hiding." He looked at me knowingly. "You know what I mean about hiding, don't you, Judy?"

"But we're not hiding anymore," I said joyfully. I went over and sat on the arm of his chair.

"That's right. We have our band."

"So who are you now?"

"I'm not telling."

I played my hands on his shoulders, like drums. "Come on," I begged.

"Just Strobe. Me. The boy inside the boy. I've discovered it's the greatest fun." He laughed. "Tea?"

I told my parents I was going to be moving out and into my own place.

"We don't want you to be alone," they said.

"I've never been alone. There was always somebody with me."

They knew I was talking about Jeffrey. But they never mentioned his name. Still. So I did.

"Jeffrey was always with me. Jeffrey. My brother. Your son. Jeffrey."

My parents looked at one another. My mother shook her head. My father said, "I can't."

"Jeffrey," I said again.

My mother closed her eyes. "Jeffrey," she said to my father.

"Jeffrey," he whispered back at her.

I put my arms around both of them. "And Judy," I said.

"And Judy. Jeffrey and Judy. Judy and Jeffrey. Our children."

"Always together," I said.

"Yes, always together."

So our family began to heal.

* * *

I didn't tell Mark what Nick had told Mr. Lieberman to tell me to tell Mark.

Instead I started to ask him a question. I said, "Mark, there's something I've always wanted to know. So I hope you don't mind—"

"Shakespeare," he said.

He was visiting me in my new loft. There was hardly any furniture. We hung out on a mattress on the floor. We weren't lovers yet. But we were very good friends. And we grew closer every day.

"There's Shakespeare." I pointed to his guitar. "But that doesn't answer my question."

He picked up the guitar and said to me as he tuned it, "I wrote down my first song. Shakespeare."

"The name of your song is Shakespeare? You named it after your guitar?"

"No. The words are from Shakespeare."

"To be or not to be?" I joked.

"Do you want to hear it or don't you want to hear it?"

"No, I don't want to hear it. At least not until you let me ask you my question. I said there's something I always wanted to know. So—"

Mark started to sing. It was a beautiful song. Slow and old-fashioned. It wasn't for the band. It wasn't for a record. It was just for me.

The man that hath no music in himself,
Nor is not moved with concord of sweet sounds,

279

Is fit for treasons, stratagems, and spoils;
The motions of his spirit are dull as night,
And his affections dark as Erebus;
Let no such man be trusted.—Mark the music.